Dear Aunt Lou,

I hope you enjoy reading this mystery story written by Sierra, my oldest grandchild (Jennifer's daughter). I'm glad we've been able to do a little visiting the last few days.

Love you!
Sue

Wolfsbane Series Book 1-Table of Contents

Prologue

Chapter 1: Newcomers

Chapter 2: Victor

Chapter 3: Secrets

Chapter 4: Dreaded

Chapter 5: Hunter

Chapter 6: Legend

Chapter 7: Trapped

Chapter 8: Rescue

Chapter 9: Transformation

Chapter 10: Hybrid

Chapter 11: Question

Chapter 12: Missing

Chapter 13: Realization

Chapter 14: Choose

Chapter 15: Responsibility

Chapter 16: Homecoming

Chapter 17: Prisoner

Chapter 18: Enemy

Chapter 19: Alpha

Epilogue

Prologue
-Anika

I can hear the snow crunch under my bare feet as I run, I run as fast as I can. I try to leave my past behind me, but it always seems to follow me. I can never escape it. Now my father is dead, my mother disappeared, and now only my best friend, Xander, and I are running in the forest together trying to escape the horrible things that follow us. I'm terrified, something stirs within me: the animal inside me is clawing its way to the surface. I force it back into its cage before it takes control. We were betrayed and exiled into the one place we won't live for long. There is no one to save us, we aren't sure we can even save ourselves.

    I duck under a branch, it scratches my face and I bleed a little. Adrenaline is the only thing keeping me going now. My breathing is hurried and I pick up speed. The beating of my heart is the only noise I hear other than the footsteps of our pursuers. Memories flash in my mind: a copper knife pressed against Xander's throat, one of my peers with a gun pointed at my wounded father, a figure following me through the woods. I shake my head to rid the memory from my mind and focused on running. I hate that boys are faster than girls. Xander is way faster than I am despite the fact that I am sprinting.

  The footsteps behind me are becoming louder and more persistent. I know that there are more of them than I originally thought. I don't know how much longer I can keep running, my legs are going numb. I look at Xander who is in the lead. He jumps over a log but I don't see it in time. My shin hits the frozen log and I fall on my face. I'm cold, tired, starving, and now I'm angry, why do I always trip over stupid logs? Xander slides to a stop and runs over to me, but it's too late. The creatures surround us but, for once, I'm not worried. I let the beast out of the cage. I look up at Xander slowly; he takes a step back from me feeling uneasy. I swallow my own fear and let it take over. They deserve this; they will regret everything they've done.

Chapter 1: Newcomers
-Anika

"It's been several weeks now." my best friend, Lani says as we walk into the adjoined gymnasium/auditorium for a mystery assembly. "I know. The whole town seems to be holding its breath. Everyone knows another attack is sure to happen soon." I say glancing at several of my teachers who look nervous and anxious. "Do you think that's what the assembly is about?" she asks, tugging on her long dirty blonde hair nervously.

"I don't know, but we're about to find out." The lights dim as we sit down on the bleachers and the spot light turns our attention to Nicki Rune, a blonde, beautiful, blue eyed head cheerleader who happens to double as the student body president. Lani and I roll our eyes as she skips to the center of the stage and does a back hand spring. All of the guys in school, and all ten cheerleaders cheer on their head cheerleader enthusiastically.

"Welcome students of Wolfsbane High! We have had a very exciting thing happen recently! After seventy years, a new family has moved into that dreadful Brennus lot in town! Yes, I know that house has had some issues in the past but they did some refurbishing and the house looks quite nice now. Without further adieu, let's bring out the new students!" Nicki smiles and claps over excitedly.

"What's got her in such a cheery mood?" I ask suspiciously narrowing my eyes in distrust. Sure, Nicki is the school's head cheerleader, but she is certainly not peppy or sweet. She tries to rule the school ruthlessly and intimidates everyone except my best friend Lani, my friend Melanie, her brother Kyle, and me. Lani and I aren't the kind of girls to get pushed around. Lani is bossy at times and hates to be told what to do and what to think. Her brother Kyle is the same way. I'm less uptight about things, but I don't like when people try to control me. If someone tries to tell me what to do I will tell them that I don't want to, what my opinion of the situation is, and I will not budge. I sometimes drive Lani crazy with how stubborn I can be.

    Lani shrugs, "I heard the new family has a really hot son. The whole package some girls' say. I guess he's okay, well, he's got abs at least." Lani says as if it's no big deal. Here, everyone has strong abs from working hard out in the fields and farming. Yep, we are a farming town and the only people that had cars were the small police force which consisted of five men and the town's Mayor. We were a pretty fit little town. The spot light turned to two teenage boys walking to the center of the gym and that's when I first see Alexander and Mason Uriel.

    Alexander is a senior, the overconfident, sporty, attractive, annoying jock type that is totally full of them selves. That doesn't surprise me at all. I could have guessed it just from looking at him. He's tall, about five foot- eleven, his skin is a lighter olive tone and he is very handsome. His dark hair is long enough to cover the tips of his ears, has high cheek bones, a chiseled jaw, eyes that look gold with emerald green flecks that sparkle in the sunlight, his smile could melt a girl's insides, and as Lani had said, his slightly tight muscle shirt showed that he had good size biceps, abs and his shorts showed off his strong calf muscles.

"Hello, fellow Wolves! I'm Alexander Uriel, but I prefer to be called Xander. But I'm sure most of you already knew that." he chuckles; the girls all giggle with him while Lani and I make soft gagging noises. He seems to be soaking up all the attention he possibly can. I roll my eyes through it, watching him would give any sane girl butterflies but the 'butterflies' I feel are just making me nauseous. I know I won't be able to stand him and his snobby attitude. "… and this is my brother Mason, say hi bro!" his brother waves and smiles shyly before tucking his hands into his pockets.

Mason is less of a show off and he seems a lot nicer than his brother. He's an inch shorter than Xander and has thick brown hair with some natural highlights. He seems to be at least a year younger than Xander so I guess he is a junior, which would mean we were in the same grade. It would be nice to have another junior in the school.

Our school isn't very big; it's about the size of an average Elementary School. This years graduating class will be about ten students. That's how many we seniors we have, including Xander. The school has a total of fifty kids, so two kids moving in is the most interesting thing that can happen in our small school- so interesting that we are having an assembly to welcome the new kids. In my opinion it's a lame excuse to waste class time, but apparently Nicki and the administration thought it was a good idea. Soon they stop talking about themselves and the assembly finally ends. I turn to Lani, who is braiding her blonde hair, clearly bored out of her mind. "So what do you think? You know, about them?" We stand up and grab our school bags. I look at the new comers as all the cheerleaders go to welcome them and all the desperate guys went to pawn for Nicki's attention and thought about how pathetic it looks.

"They seem nice, but I doubt they'll last three weeks here. That house they're occupying usually empties in about two weeks due to the incidents and strange noises there." Lani shrugs.

"Yeah, I guess you're right, unless that pretty boy and his brother can really fight, they won't be here long." I reply as we exit the gym and head to our first period classes.

I have chemistry first. I come to the door and sit in my normal seat in the back of the room next to the window. The bell rang indicating that class had begun. The chemistry teacher doubles as our school's Football coach, teaching his two favorite subjects, sometimes at the same time- using football analogies to explain atoms and nuclear behaviors that only he understands.

Five minutes into Coach Dastin's lecture about atoms, Xander walks in creating a big entrance with none other than the head cheerleader herself and her personal wannabe: Dana. "Here's your first class Xander." Nicki says flirtatiously. "Thanks for helping me find it ladies." Xander replies, winking. The cheerleaders giggle and Coach Dastin and the rest of the class stare in shock, watching Nicki flirt is in a word, disturbing. "Ah Uriel, how kind of you to join us. Take a seat and next time, be on time for class." Coach Dastin raises his eye brow at the two obnoxious cheerleaders. "Shouldn't you be in class?"

"Bye Xander!" they say at the same time, they then turn on their heels and strut off down the hallway.

"Uriel, please take a seat next to... Conall." Coach Dastin commands. My head shoots up at the sound of my last name.
Please no! My mind screams. When Xander sees me, he smiles.

"Certainly," he says as he strolls over and slides into his seat next to mine. The lecture resumes and I tried to focus but I can feel Xander's eyes on me. It makes me feel self conscious and it becomes harder to focus. After the lecture had ends we got our assignments.

"Excuse me?" Xander asks when I get to my last question on the assignment. I sigh and turn toward him slowly.

"Yes?" I ask as politely as I can manage.

"Could you give me the answers for the assignment?"

"Can't you do it yourself? Did you even listen to the lecture at all?" I ask dully.

"I tried, but," he pauses and gather his thoughts. "Can you please just give me the answers?"

"No, you can't cheat off me!" I whisper fiercely.

"Not cheat! Just give me clues." he whispers back smiling innocently. I pause and think about it. I know he won't leave me alone until I help him somehow. I sigh and push my notes in his direction so he can use them.

"Next time, come on time and use your own notes for the assignments." I say as I get up to turn my paper in.

"I will thanks." He says halfheartedly followed by a mischievous smirk on his face.

~   ~   ~

I find Lani at our locker after school. I tell her about what happened during first period. "Oh that really sucks, I'm sorry. He definitely acts like a jerk. He's in my history class and he distracted the teacher so we didn't get through the lesson." She explains as we start walking home from school.

"It's okay; it looks like we'll just have to deal with him and his annoying personality." I sigh.

"Hey guys!" a blonde haired, skinny figure of a boy catches up to us yells.

"Hey Bro," Lani smiles.

"Have you guys met the new kids yet? Mason and I are buds."

"Oh, well I've met Xander but not Mason." I say as Mason approaches us.

"Mason, this is my sister and her friend Anika. Anika this is Mason." Kyle says introducing us, we shake hands. "Nice to meet you," He says smiling.

"Like wise." I reply with a polite smile, already deciding I like him way more than his snob of a brother. We continue walking when Xander catches up to us. He talks with only Kyle and Mason, and ignores me and Lani which I'm fine with. They start laughing and joking around as Lani and I roll our eyes at their immaturity when we hear it: The blood curdling screams that turn our bones to ice and causes us all to freeze where we stand.

Chapter 2: Victor
-Xander

My first official day in a new area, and it takes a horrifying turn. Every one of us stiffens; the two girls with us look absolutely terrified. We run toward the sound of the screams, and that's when I see it. I feel numb and stop running immediately; my stomach feels sickly as we approach it. The scene before me is gruesome and devastating. There was some bizarre animal attack. A teen lay on his back staring lifelessly up at the gray sky. He is covered in strange deep bite and claw marks on his arms and legs and thick scratches on his chest. He is bleeding profusely. Kyle's sister falls to her knees in shock, struggling to breathe.

"Not another one," the girl from my chemistry class whimpers putting her hands over her mouth hopelessly and shaking her head.

"They've attacked us again. That's the third time this month now. They're getting braver." Kyle says worriedly.

"We've got to get away from here. They were hunting him so they can't be far from here. I'm alerting the police. They'll come get Victor to a hospital," Kyle's sister says pulling out her phone.

"Lani, it's too late. He's dead, and we will be too if we stay here. Let's go." Anika says turning away from the horrendous sight and walking back the way we came, Lani follows her, as does Kyle.

"We can't just leave him!" I shout at her, Anika turns and glares at me, tears brimming in her eyes.

"You think this isn't hard for me? I actually knew Victor! I grew up with him! But there is nothing we can do to save him. The poison has already entered his blood stream and he has bled to death! It's too late for him! If you want to stay then that's your decision, but you'll end up just like him. You are no exception to them." she shouts rather tensely, tears spilling from her eyes.

"Wait, you know what attacked him don't you! What was it?" I demand, but she just turns on her heel and walks the other direction, everyone else following her. Mason looks at me, and then to them, he gets out his phone.

"I'm still calling the police but they're right. It isn't safe here right now." He dials 9-1-1 and jogs up to catch up to them putting the phone up to his ear. I grunt angrily, tightening my fists and glaring at my chemistry partner's back until she is out of sight. I then turn my glance to the woods, then back at where the group had been walking away from the crime scene. I stay put until I hear the sirens of an ambulance. I start walking toward where the group had left. I turn around to get one last look at the poor victim, but when I look back- Victor's body is missing.

~   ~   ~

After I discover Victor is gone I sprint home without looking back. My heart is racing and my hands are shaking. *He was right there, dead, unmoving... and then he was just... gone. But how?* I wonder. My dog, Darla, comes to greet me when I open the front door of my house, her tail wagging and she chuffs at me with excitement. I can tell she missed me. I kneel down and scratch behind her ears. She's a hunting dog, half chocolate Labrador and half Pointer. A beautiful mix of both: looks exactly like a chocolate lab but had a patch of white fur on her chest and some on her toes like she has socks on her feet, and her eyes like mine, are golden. Her behavior is that of a loyal Lab that loves to hunt. She's my best friend. I smile at her, I missed her too.

Today had just been strange for me and I can't make sense of it all. First, a girl I think is pretty has rolls her eyes at me as if I am an inconvenience to her in chemistry class. Everyone else had been so nice to me but for some reason it bothers me that my chemistry partner seems to view me as an annoyance or burden. Then she just left that Victor guy to die only to have him randomly disappear- and to disappear that fast. I had only walked five steps before I turned around to see that he was gone from where he lay only a few seconds earlier. How can that possibly happen?

My curiosity gets the better of me. I put Darla on her leash and run back to the site of the attack with her. There is now crime scene tape around where Victor's body has been which is marked with a small puddle of dry blood. There are no cop cars or anything else showing the police had been there. *They aren't even doing an investigation or a search? What's wrong with this town?* I think as I duck under the crime tape. I let Darla get a whiff of Victor's scent then let her track it. I follow her into the woods. We wander for a while; dark clouds hang over heads threatening rain on us.

    The thick trees loom over head, and I begin to think about the huge differences of this odd town in Maine that my parents randomly chose to move to that is so far away from my beloved hometown in California. Trying to loose the feeling I have that I am being watched and followed. But my mind keeps playing tricks on me, seeing shadows in the corner of my eye. I move cautiously, keeping Darla close. That's when she stops and sniffs the air, begins sniffing in circles, then she sits down and whimpers as if she is confused. She lay down and covers her head with her paws; she has given up and can't follow his scent any farther… as if he doesn't exist anymore. This puzzles me. If someone had moved his body and buried him she'd be able to find him. I bend down and pat Darla on the head told her she was a good girl and give her a dog treat. That's when she suddenly jumps up and starts growling and barking at the trees looking seriously angry.

    I look around, but I can't see what has spooked her except for the moving shadows my mind was making up. I stand up and realize I've been out here in the woods for too long and it was time to go home. I begin walking and hear a twig snap behind me. I turn around to see Darla snap at a hooded figure that disappears like a shadow with inhuman speed. I take off running; Darla growls but follows my lead. I have no idea what just happened, but inside I am shaken up and slightly terrified. I don't stop running until we are out of the woods and can't see edge of the forest from the town.

Chapter 3: Secrets
- Anika

Everyone is tense over the next week of school. We have gotten word that Victor's body was no where to be found. It brings lots of uneasiness and fear to town. But no one seems to be affected more by Victor's disappearance than Xander is. He seems to be upset all week. He doesn't speak to anyone, not even his brother. His angry temper is even more annoying than his cocky one. Toward the end of the week he starts asking tons of dangerous questions about Victor's death and the woods, and when people don't answer him, he'd ask someone else or just fold his arms and glare at the chalk board at the front of the room during class.

"Anika, please. No one will answer my questions. I'm getting impatient and when I reach the point I will go into the woods and hunt whatever attacked Victor myself." This scares me, I'm not sure if he was being serious so I decide to ignore him. He sits, glaring at the chalk board for about five minutes until I just can't take it anymore.

He is acting like a four- year-old and it is driving me insane. "I know Victor's disappearance is shocking to you. But you barely knew him... You barely know anyone in town." I try to say in a concerned, non-irritable voice.

"I just don't get it. A poor guy gets attacked and then goes missing. He was badly wounded and no one even checked to see if he was alive. Maybe if we got there sooner we could have saved him. But you just left him. You left him there in a hurry without a care in the world. It was cruel; I told you we should have stayed with him, but no. You were too much of a coward to do that. Now he's gone and no one cares. They didn't even look that hard to try to find him. You act like it's a normal thing. What's wrong with this sick, twisted town?" He whispers harshly glaring at me angrily, I'm stunned.

He has just insulted me and my town. I shouldn't be surprised but I just wasn't expecting it. I can't find anything to say. I feel like I should be angry but I just feel numb. He is right, our town has become used to the attacks and we block all feeling for when we lose someone. We are somewhat heartless, but being raised in this town, you have to be. People disappear often due to attacks. When I finally find my voice, I speak.

"Look, you don't know these people. You don't know me, so you have no right to judge. The town has been this way longer than anyone can remember. When you grow up here you learn that there was nothing we could do for people in Victor's situation. People here get attacked if they aren't careful, especially when they are alone. Normally we only get three attacks a year but Victor's was the tenth this year alone. Ten people gone, that is a lot. Something is changing and everyone is scared. I am, and so are you." I wait for his reaction.

"I am not scared." He says half laughing, half angrily as if suggesting he is afraid is insulting. "Everyone gets scared, especially about what's unknown to them. The cowards are the ones who say they aren't." I reply stubbornly folding my arms.

"Believe me, I'm not scared." He laughs as a matter-of-factly, while gripping his pencil so hard that I think he is going to break it. I raise an eyebrow, unconvinced.

"I'm serious. I'm just confused and frustrated by the whole thing. The day Victor was attacked we were at the scene and you left. And when I decided to leave I turned around to see the guy one last time but-" he pauses and looks around, suddenly looking nervous.

"But?" I urge him on. His gold eyes grow dark when he recalls this memory.

"When I looked back his body was gone. It was like he just vanished. I know there was no way he could have gotten up. He was dead so there is no way he could have. I only found a puddle of blood marking the spot he was in." Xander shakes his head and I freeze, staring at him in terror. "What?" he asks.

My mouth won't work; it's like the connection from my brain to my body is broken. My mind is buzzing but I can't move. I swallow the sheer terror that prohibits my voice from speaking.

"They took him. And we were that close to them. They didn't even make any noise. They could have grabbed one of us," I blurt out quickly my panic rising and I can't seem to breathe.

"Hush, Anika calm down." Xander says quietly, putting his finger on my lips. His touch calms me down instantly, chills creep up my arms, and I gaze into his pure golden eyes. *What's happening to me? Why do I suddenly feel so safe? Stop staring at him!* I think and tare my gaze from his. "That's not all," he confesses removing his finger from my lips, my eyes widen. *There's more?* I think, my mind racing. "After that I went home and I took my dog, Darla, to where Victor was attacked. She caught his scent and I followed her into the woods." He says as if it is a normal thing he does on the weekends.

"You did what!" I yell in surprise. The whole class turns to look at us. I blush and slump in my chair while Xander smiled casually, enjoying his new found attention. Eventually people get bored of watching us and return to their work.

"Are you crazy? You can't go into the woods! Especially not the evening after an attack just happened!" I whispered hurriedly, He just rolls his eyes.

"Relax, I never found anything anyway. But that's why I'm so frustrated. He didn't leave any trace of his existence. His scent vanished just as quickly as he did. Darla was acting strange though, barking at trees and random things where there was no one there." He explains, truly puzzled. I can't believe what I'm hearing.

"You could have been attacked! They could have gotten you and killed you! What's wrong with you! Everyone knows not to go into the woods. That's suicide!" I whisper, his brows furrow.

"Well, I'm obviously still here so nothing killed me. Who is this they you people keep mentioning?" he asks irritated. I look around cautiously, unsure about how to address this question. I know if I don't tell him he'll try to find out himself and end up getting himself killed. But talking about them is against the rules in town because it causes panic and fear within town's members. I can get in huge trouble for this, but someone needs to tell him. I lean in closer when I am sure no one is listening or paying attention to us. He does the same.

"Alright, you deserve to know. But you have to promise that you'll never pull a stupid stunt like going into the woods alone again. You have to promise." I say seriously looking deep into his eyes to make sure he knew the importance of the promise.

"I promise."

"Okay, they are called," I hesitate for a moment. I am about to break a town rule by talking about them. His eyes plead with mine to tell him. He did promise so I have to follow through with my end of the deal, I sigh.

"They are called Dreads." I whisper in such a low voice that I'm not sure if he heard me. He looks even more confused.

"What are Dre-," I interrupt him before he could finish.

"Hush! We're not supposed to talk about them!" I whisper covering his mouth with my hand to silence him. I pause and realize my hand is touching his soft, warm lips. Butterflies explode in my stomach and I drop my hand onto my lap, feeling the imprint of his lips on my palm. My face grows hot and I turn away from him. "I'll tell you more where there are less people around. Meet me by the front doors after school if you want to learn more." I see him nod out of the corner of my eye and the bell rings; we stand and leave the class room not looking at each other. I can't believe what I have just told him or the fact that I touched his mouth with my hand and is now burning. He is getting dangerous information, if only he knew what he is getting himself into.

Chapter 4: Dreaded
- Xander

I wait outside the school doors impatiently looking at every girl's face to see if it was Anika's. "Looking for me?" She chuckles a few feet away from me. I smile feeling foolish and wonder how long she had been standing there. She holds her hands nervously in front of her; I look at her hands which remind me of when she covered my mouth to silence me in chemistry this morning. My face began to feel hot from the memory. I push the thought from my head and approach her.

"Yep," I say putting on a broad smile after pushing my hand through my hair as if to push away my embarrassment. She smirks and starts walking toward the part of town where the houses are.

"Oh, wait! I promised Coach Dastin I'd talk to him about football tryouts after school. Would you mind coming with me?" I plead, she sighs.

"Fine, just don't be too long."

She follows me to the football field and sits on the bleachers pulling out a book to read while I jog over to Coach Dastin. The team is already on the football field doing warm ups. "Hey Coach! Can I talk to you for a sec?" I ask smiling.

"Uriel! Of course you can! I was wondering when you'd get here. Ready to suit up? You and Marcus will be competing for who gets the quarterback position!" Coach Dastin seems excited to have a good player on his team. He found out I was the star quarterback last year at my school in California and that my team had been undefeated. He has begged me to tryout for the team since I moved in.

"Oh, I thought that tryouts were tomorrow. I still have to get the forms to my parents to sign. Could it be possible to do it tomorrow?" I ask hoping it wasn't an inconvenience. I actually got my parents to sign the forms a long time ago. I just know if I don't go with Anika, she'll never tell me about the Dreads. The Coach thinks about it for a little bit.

"Alright, just don't forget them tomorrow."

"I won't Coach, thank you!"

When I turn around I see that the cheerleaders are coming onto the track to practice and some of them are eyeing Anika.

"Oh look girls, it's the Bookworm. What are you doing here at a cheerleading practice? Wishing you were one of us?" I hear Dana ask Anika, the cheerleaders surround her, sneering.

"I'm not here to spy on you. I'm here with an acquaintance to help him with homework. I could care less about both football and cheer. They are just a waste of time to me. Now if you wouldn't mind moving your big head out of the way, you're kinda blocking the sun and it makes it harder to read." Anika says looking Dana right in the eyes without fear.

"Well, well, well- an acquaintance? Is he on the Football team? Mind if we meet him? Or does he not exist?" Nicki spits at her, folding her arms. Anika turns her glare to Nicki; I begin to walk faster towards them, I know this won't end well.

"For your information, I have no interest in cheerleading, or sports, or football players. Just leave me alone. Your insecurity spreads like a disease," Anika says, "and that's something I sure don't want to catch." Anika sees me as I reach the bleachers; she stands, smiles at the cheerleaders smugly, and walks over to me.

"You've got to be joking, Xander?" Nicki laughs in disbelief,

"Hello Nicki, it's nice to see you. Come on Anika, let's go." I say walking away from the field and Anika keeps my pace. I'm silently impressed with how she handled the situation. She wasn't pushed around and she stood up for herself. Not what I expected from her.

~   ~   ~

The walk to her house is quiet. We both walk in silence for a while, she looks straight ahead, her arms swinging back and fourth, one hand clutches a book. I match her pace. "So, you're not a big fan of cheerleaders are you?" I ask, she looks at me in surprise.

"No not really. I mean, I'm not by any means jealous. Nicki and I have never gotten along. Our families have always disagreed. I guess it's just the way it's always been. I don't mind the cheerleaders; I just don't like being treated like dirt. I'm not going to stand there and take it. I'm going to dish it out as well. If they can't take it they should just leave me alone. I've done nothing to them. I don't understand why they feel like they have to control me." She explains, kicking a rock on the ground and watching it bounce around ahead of us.

"I understand, I hate when people try to make me feel worthless." Anika chuckles softly at this. "What? You think I don't know how it feels?"

"Xander, I doubt you even know what rejection feels like." She says, shaking her head.

"You think I've never been rejected?" I ask incredulously.

"What I think doesn't matter." Is all she says back to me.

That's when we turn to her house and approach the front door. She opens the door and invites me inside; her mother is there washing dishes.

"Hello Mother, this is Xander Uriel. He's new and needed help with some school work. Is it okay if I tutor him in Dad's office?" Anika asks in a strange voice.

Her mother looks up from the dishes to me.

"Oh, hello Xander. I heard a new family moved in. I'm Carolyn Conall, Anika's Mom." She holds out her hand and I shake it.

"Nice to meet you Mrs.Conall." I smile at her and she smiles back.

"You are welcome to use your father's study Anika as long as you don't touch anything you aren't supposed to." Mrs. Conall says to her daughter. They exchange a look of understanding and then Anika walks into the basement and I follow. I wonder what the look they exchanged means as we enter her father's study.

Their basement is cut in half, a wall with a metal safe door hiding one half, the other half is a library with chairs combined with an office desk. "My father is

Wolfsbane's deputy and detective, that's why the basement is his study; he brings work home with him a lot."

"That makes sense." I reply as she offers me a seat on a rather surprisingly comfortable reading sofa.

"Okay, so you want to learn more about... them. I only know things about them from books and stories so," Anika turns then walks to the bookshelves and extracts a book from the neatly organized shelves of books and blows off the dust that covered it like a blanket. It looks like it hasn't been used in a long time. She walks over and places the book in my hands.

It has no title and the cover is made of thick old leather. I open it carefully and study its yellow tattered pages. It has illustrations that are very detailed and long explanations depicting each mythical creature clearly. There are Trolls, Ogres, Phantoms, Sea Monsters, the Moth-man, a strange half man- half bat creature called a Knight, an angel looking creature with hawks wings and piercing fierce eyes called a Fowl, and some interesting creature called a Slayer that is closely related to the Werewolf.

I turn the page once more to find a creature I don't recognize. It has scaled skin, long hideous talons on its hands and feet, a pointed nose, sharp snake fangs and bright yellow and red cat's eyes. It was standing on two legs but hunched over because of its huge muscle mass. The surprising part is that it doesn't have a tail. It was covered in a black cloak and had a snarling angry look on its face. In one word, this creature is disturbing. I look at the name of this monster at the top of the page. It reads, 'The Dreaded'. Along with the drawing and the Beast's name there is a description:

>*'The Dreaded ones are hunters. They stalk their prey then attack when it's at the most vulnerable point and drain them of their blood. They don't like to fight but will put up a fight if necessary. They have excellent camouflage skills, almost like a chameleon their scales can change to blend with the environment and they can go almost anywhere in the forest unseen. They are ten times stronger and faster than the average human. Their claws and retractable fangs have a sort of paralyzing poison that causes their prey to bleed faster. Their reflexes are unparalleled. They have only one weakness that we know of, and that is copper. Their only known enemy is the Slayer. The Dreaded are extremely dangerous and impossible to escape. They are*

more dangerous than ogres or trolls combined.'

I look at the picture again, this time getting goose bumps. Its eyes seem to pierce my soul. I shake my head and think *she can't really believe this stuff can she?*

I turn the book towards Anika and say, "So they're basically vampire lizards."

"No, they are Dreads. Vampires don't exist. Dreads can be in the sunlight and can go wherever they please and eat anything they want when they want. They aren't intelligent like humans, they are smart, but they are animals that hunt to stay alive. They don't just drink blood, they're carnivores. They eat the whole carcass, and they don't live forever, they die of old age as well as humans do. They're animals, but they are terrifying, smart, well hidden animals that eat people." She explains, I sit and ponder this for a moment before replying.

"I'm not sure if it's just me, but if and this ugly thing and I was competing to see who had the most attractive face, I would win hands down! But that's just my opinion, what do you think?" I smile, holding the book the same level as my face so she can see the picture and compare it. Anika looks from my face to the picture, and then smirks.

"Hmmm, I'm not sure. I think right now it's a tie."

"What? No way! You've got to be joking!" I say in disbelief, frowning and acting hurt by her words. Suddenly her face lit up and she laughs. Instantly I feel embarrassed and self conscious- which was a shock. I'm not used to feeling that way. But I also feel like her laugh opened her up a little more. She isn't as stiff as I thought she was, and she is surprisingly beautiful. She has thick, wavy, long brown hair, olive toned skin, a perfectly white, straight toothed smile, and beautiful green eyes. Her laugh is also quite cute as well, and I find myself smiling and laughing along with her.

After the laughing subsides she watches me smiling, and trying to be serious again-it isn't working.

"Anyway, you found it: the monster that terrorizes us all. Well in this town anyway," she sighs.

"Wow, how do they know they look like this?" I ask in amazement, her eyes widen.

"Um, well. I already showed you a lot about them and," She pauses and glances around nervously. I give her my best puppy dog eyes I can manage. No girl can resist them, no matter how stubborn they are. This takes her by surprise for a second but then she rolls her eyes at me. "Fine, if you want to learn more, just read this."

She reaches into the back of the self and removes a couple books revealing a safe hidden inside the bookshelf. My eyes widen, her surprises never seem to cease. Her fingers move speedily on the dial. After unlocking it, she extracts a book and shoves a random book into the safe. After that, she relocks it and puts back the books she had removed from the bookshelf.

She walks over to me and shoves the smaller book into my arms quickly but carefully. "Please return it as soon as you're done reading it. I mean immediately after, do you understand? People would kill for this book. Do not let anyone know you have it." She looks right into my eyes without hesitation; I knew she is dead serious.

This just piques my curiosity about the book I held in my hands even more.

"Okay, I promise."

"I'm holding you to that promise." She says then her mother calls her name causing her to jump. "Coming!" She says, shoving the book in my bag, zipping it and shoving it into my arms then pushing me up the stairs quickly and out the door.

"Thank you," I try to say but by then she closed the door and leaves me on her porch alone with my backpack and the mysterious book inside of it.

Chapter 5: Hunter
-Anika

I close the door quickly as I push Xander out of it, practically slamming it in his face. After, I lock it and then lean against the door, sliding down it until I was sitting on the floor. *What am I doing? Am I losing my mind? Giving my Great, Great, Great Grandfather's journal to a complete stranger! And for what? Because he had a handsome face and irresistible golden eyes?* I shake my head and rub my temples. "Anika? Where are you?" My mother calls. I take a deep breath and get myself to my feet.

I have to start avoiding Xander. He is asking way too many dangerous questions and dragging me in the middle of it. If he keeps asking them, we will both be in trouble, or worse. My parents will have my head if they knew I lent him the Journal. That book no one outside of my family has seen- until today that is.

I walk into the kitchen to find my mother has started making cookies. These cookies where gluten and soy free: they consisted of peanut butter, sugar, and an egg. They were that easy to make, you just mix them up and put them in the oven to bake. I never understood my mother. She is so into health, fitness, and eating healthy ever since I was a young child. I admire her for it; it seems to be a hobby of hers. She is always experimenting with cooking healthy foods and smoothies and such. Miraculously most of the things she makes actually turn out to be pretty tasty, but I don't like these particular types of cookies because I hate peanut butter. I make a face as I enter the kitchen to be greeted by the scent of her ingredients. My mother laughs when she sees my face.

"You called?" I ask, plugging my nose to escape the odor. My mother smiles at me, knowing my distaste for anything peanut related.

"Yes, sweetheart. I was wondering if Xander wanted to try any of my cookies. Where is he? You didn't leave him in your father's dungeon did you?" She asks raising an eyebrow, I shake my head.

"He had to leave earlier than expected." I say unplugging my nose, trying to ignore the smell that fills the kitchen.

"Well that's a bummer. I was hoping he'd try this recipe. Maybe he'll come back soon." She says setting the pan of cookies into the oven.

"I doubt that," I say under my breath. The phone rings right after my mother set the timer, I answer it- It's my father. "Anika, grab your bow and you're camping bag, we're going hunting tonight. See you in five minutes." he then hung up the phone. I hung up the wall phone and smile at my mom.

I skip into my room grabbing my favorite black, leather hoodie and slip on my black Converse shoes, then run down to my father's study. I put in the code that unlocks the safe to my father's armory. It takes up more than half the basement. It's filled with diverse weapons, which include daggers, machetes, handguns, Scar H Assault Rifle, a shot gun, lots of other weapons I don't know the names of, and of course, my sleek black bow and specially crafted copper tipped arrows. Every bullet, dagger, machete, and all of the tips of my arrows were made of the same thing: copper.

    My smile broadens as I sling my quiver full of arrows over my shoulder and pick up my bow. I always find myself looking forward to the Fridays that I went hunting with my father. We go hunting every other month, but this year, for some reason, we have gone hunting more than usual. I head up the stairs after locking my father's armory safe door tightly behind me.

    My father pulls up to the house in his cop car, kisses my mother and whispers in her ear. She nods and hands him a cookie and kisses his cheek and hugs me and tells me to be careful. That's how it usually goes when we went off hunting. I hop in the driver's seat of my father's black Dodge Ram truck and he hopped into the passenger's seat. My father smiles as I start the engine and back out of the driveway. We go up the usual road we take and I drive us to our normal parking spot at the town's abandoned shooting range.

    We grab our gear, my bow and quiver full of arrows, and my dad's lucky handgun and dagger he always has in his truck. We lock up the truck and disappear in the midst of the woods together as the sun begins to set. We slow to a walk and I nock an arrow on my bow, we hear movement up ahead. I look at my father with serious eyes. 'How many?' I mouth, he held up four fingers. This was going to be an easy weekend. We split up, I took the right side and he took the left. Now you might be thinking we are hunting deer or elk but you would be wrong. We are not normal hunters- we're monster hunters. We hunt the Dreads to keep them from attacking people in town; it's like monster population control.

    Our plan is always simple; my father distracts them while I shoot them all from behind. My father makes lots of noise, now I can see them, they aren't being careful like they normally are. They are vicious, smart, and always hungry creatures. They all sniff the air and follow the sounds my father is making. The distraction is perfect; I shoot my first arrow and nock another in seconds shooting another and another.

    The last one disappears from my view. I look around trying to catch a glimpse of it; I turn around only to be face to face with it. The bald Dread hisses in my face, showing its hideous yellow, snake like fangs. Its nasty breath fills my nostrils, its scales seem to protrude from its face and it lunges at me. My instincts kick in wasting no time; I pull the copper dagger from by back pocket and stab the monster in front of me. Pushing the dagger further and further into its rib cage until I twist it and its yellow eyes darken indicating it was no longer alive.

    It slumps over and I push it so it falls on its back in front of me, freeing my dagger from its scaly body. It seems to take forever for me to catch my breath. I have never been that close to a Dread before. At least it was dead now along with the other ones. My father came up behind me and put his hand on my shoulder. We both stare at the Dread I had just killed. "And that my daughter is how a true Hunter does it. I'm proud of you! I didn't even have to intervene." He says smiling. I try to smile, but my nerves won't allow it. I just stare at its lifeless body. "Come on, lets burn the bodies or their pack will smell them and trace them to us." He commands turning serious again. I help him stack them into a pile and he sets it on fire. I'm still in shock from the too close encounter with the Dread. The rest of the hunting trip was a blur, and we don't see anymore Dreads.

By Sunday morning we pack up and head home. My father drove, the drive home was silent mostly. I know my father understood that the experience of being that close to a Dread for the first time had shaken me; luckily he is kind about it and doesn't give me a hard time. After a few failed attempts to start a conversation he sighs and tells me something that changed my current perspective.

"Anika, Honey. I can see that seeing a Dread like that can throw you off balance for a bit. I remember my first experience face to face with a Dread, and I got used to it. But there is something you must learn. We always find strength when we least expect it. When we think all is lost, strength will come in abundance, as long as you know what's truly important. Do you know why I hunt those monsters, Anika?" he asks, when I don't reply he continues any way. "I hunt because I want to keep you and your mother safe. It ends up helping the community as well. I need you to learn to protect yourself from them because I know there will come a day that I won't be there to keep you safe."

I realize what my father has been thinking. He must see my fear of being face to face with a Dread irrational. I have killed plenty of those monsters before. My family has been descended from Monster Hunters as far back as we can trace our ancestry. I have my trusty bow so I've never had to do hand to hand combat against a Dread, they have always been farther away, never closer than ten feet.

When we get home it's late, I go to bed and try to get some rest, but can't sleep because every time I close my eyes all I can see is the Dread hissing in my face. The next morning, I know I'm going to have a rough week ahead of me. I had gotten no sleep last night, and I had a feeling that Xander isn't going to make it any easier for me.

Chapter 6: Legend
- Xander

Anika is acting very strange on today. She looks exhausted and when I talk to her she ignores me. I try not to let it bother me, but it does. After Chemistry was over, which never seemed to end, I head to all of my other classes. My head full of questions I was dying to ask Anika. *What about this book was so important? Why does everyone believe that there really are monsters in the woods if no one's seen them before? Could it be wolves killing the people? But how could they disappear?* During lunch I immerse myself in the stories of the mysterious book she had given me last Friday. It is strange but the entries are so detailed. I assume it was a journal, a really old one but it was preserved extremely well. Only a few entries stood out to me.

June 9, 1812

"The Dreaded seem to come out of the woods more and more since the death of our leader Clint Brennus. The new leader, Charles Dunstan doesn't seem to be doing anything to stop them. He's too drunk with power to care

what happens to the town's folk. Mangus Ulric and I have started at town militia to ward off the monsters. We can't seem to kill them with anything. They get wounded but it doesn't stop them. We keep trying but more and more are dying and people are getting worried. People want to leave because it isn't safe here anymore. I agree with them but the Mayor won't allow it. I'm not sure why he insists on staying here with so many people dying. The town won't last much longer if we stay. I'm going to keep fighting and try and convince the Charles to let us leave. I hope it goes well."

July 27, 1812
"The town was attacked today. Over half of the Militia and about ten women were dragged into the woods by the beasts. They don't seem so fond of killing their prey on the spot anymore. No one dares to go into the woods to follow. Anyone that tries never comes back. The Mayor still does nothing. Mangus, Edmund, and I have started planning on how to get out of here to safety somewhere

new. Now Charlie has gone too far with his Tyranny. We leave in about a week's time."

August 8, 1812

"They were waiting for us; the Dreaded had surrounded the town so no one could leave. It was like they knew our plan all along. They chased us back to town and killed many of us. I had a copper knife I made when I was a mere lad in me pocket. It was the only thing I had to carry in my defense after I lost my other weapon. A Dread attacked me from behind; I grasped my small copper knife and plunged it into its side. The creature hissed angrily, bearing it's fangs before falling lifeless to the ground. When the Dreaded noticed their fallen comrade they fled into the woods, hissing and growling as they went. That's when we first got to study the body of the Dreaded. We now understand its ability to hide so well and what it eats and what its weaknesses are. We have finally found a way to defeat them. Copper, we are starting to mine for some to make into weapons as of this month."

September 5, 1812

"Something is different now. The Mayor is angry and acting suspiciously. I suspect he knows more about these attacks from the Dreaded than he is telling the town. I see him leave his house late at night only to come back early in the morning. When he leaves his house he vanishes into the forest, but he always returns. What is he doing all the way out there in the forest alone? How does he avoid attacks? Something isn't right and I'm going to find out what. I'm following him tonight."

September 8, 1812

"Something is strange, I can't remember what happened the night I went into the woods after the Mayor. I woke up right on the edge of the forest unharmed by the Dreaded with blood on my fingers that was not my own. The Mayor is back at his house but I can't figure out what happened. I feel different, like I'm stronger. I'm not afraid of the Dreaded anymore. I found a bite mark on my shoulder, like some sort of animal bit me. I might be sick, but I don't feel sick. I'm not sure if I should tell the others about my injury or about the mayor. They might turn on me. I need to be careful. The Mayor is becoming strict and is now sending sacrifices into the woods to appease the Dreaded into not attacking. I do not like where this is going. Human sacrifices are barbaric. I will not stand for this."

I read all I could about the Dreads. One story stood out more than the others: The final entry of the journal. I reread it to make sure I didn't miss anything.

October 11, 1812
"They are closing in on us. The militia is seriously out numbered this time. We won't make it out alive. None of us will. I send my love to my wife and children. They will preserve the town and keep it going. I can feel the monster within me arise. I will not be who I am much longer. The Dreaded sneer at us, but

I can tell they are unsure of me..." There was a line of scribbles I couldn't read, and then it continues:

"I shall do what I must to protect my family and my town from these beasts. I'm slipping, the creature within me is trying to take control, and nothing can stop it. Not even the Dreaded. I pray that it may be enough to stop them. God save us, and please, protect my family. They-"

Then it just ends. I turn to the next page and there is nothing. Puzzled I flip through the pages one last time. I close the book and noticed something I missed before. On the leather cover there are scratch marks as if from claws. I can't understand what it means, but I know I have to lots of questions for Anika when I gave her the book back. I need answers; this whole mythical town monster thing is driving me crazy. I have to prove to them it isn't true. A monster living in those woods just isn't possible.

I head to my forth period class, football conditioning. All we do are warm ups, running, and weight lifting. After school is practice during which I'll be fighting for the position of quarterback, I don't want it but Coach Dastin insists. My head just isn't in it. My thoughts are preoccupied with questions of mythical creatures and why Anika is avoiding me. I miss a lot of the passes and get knocked to the ground a lot more than usual. I don't remember much from that practice. I know I didn't get the quarter back position, which was fine with me. I want to try being a running back anyway, less pressure that way.

    A guy named Marcus Brett got the position he wanted which was nice. He seems like the kind of guy I was likely to clash with anyway. He is a pretty big guy, large muscle mass, a little taller than I am, bright blonde hair and dark brown eyes that always seem suspicious and observant. He fit television's definition of a Jock perfectly. As did most of the team, they seem to be a pack of wolves. Close knit and loyal to their pack leader, Marcus.

    They picked me, the new kid, as the lone wolf. I wouldn't care if it didn't mean that I'm their main target in practice. They always make a play I don't know about and I'd get tackled to the ground somehow. Soon I start to catch on, I realize that I have to be aware of what they are up to and be light on my feet. I learn I can get away if I'm fast enough but sadly I'm only fast enough half of the time. When they could catch me, they make sure it hurts. I don't know what they have against me, but I manage to both stay alive and get Coach Dastin to love me.

When practice was finally over, I feel like I can breathe again. The rest of the team went into the locker rooms to change. I find it best to hang out around the field for a little while longer. It's cloudy outside and the cool wind feels nice. I decide to explore the area until I feel like I can change out of the practice pads I had on. I notice that on the north side behind the bleachers only a fence separates the school grounds from a cornfield. On the west end is the woods and the east is the soccer field and the south side is more bleachers and the school's gymnasium entrance.

After I figure I have pushed off the locker room long enough. I sigh, turn and head toward the gym. I take my time, not wanting to rush; it's peaceful to just be alone and to think. That's when I hear something unexpected from the west. I look toward the noise and see something move. I freeze, staring at the spot that I see the movement. I wait for what seems to be forever and nothing happens. I return my attention to the gym. When I get to the door, I turn around to recheck the woods. This time, there is a figure. The black cloaked figure I had seen my first day in Wolfsbane was leaning against a tree, watching me. When I blink it disappeared as quickly as it came. I open the door and hurry inside. I need to see Anika again. I have to get answers, now.

Chapter 7: Trapped

-Anika

I hate staying after school, but today I don't mind it much. They bought some new books to add to the library and they said if I helped I'd get first pick of the new selection, so I had helped eagerly. We finish faster than I thought we would. I head to the exit with my book in my hands excited to see what story had been printed on its pages. That's when I had unexpectedly run into Xander, well more like he ran into me, literally. I turn the corner only to bump into him as he left the men's locker room. It sent me tumbling toward the ground; my book flew out of my hands. Somehow he managed to catch me, and I caught my book before we both hit the ground. "I'm so sorry. I didn't see you, are you alright?" He asks helping me back on my feet. I was stunned. I was beginning to think fate wants me to run into him because the harder I try to stay away, the more I find myself with him. He looks exhausted and I can see he was starting to bruise on his arms.

"Are you okay?" I ask lightly touching his new bruises on impulse. My fingers seem to hum with electricity when they touched him.

"I'm fine. I guess I'm just a clumsy running back." He laughs, but the sad, tense look in his eyes tells me he's laying. The last running back never had bruises like this after the first practice.

"Xander, that's not normal. Either you bruise extremely easily, or they hurt you pretty bad." I say looking at him with genuine concern. *Why do I care? The cheerleaders and other girls will be fussing over him about this. I'm not like them.* I try to clear my head but something inside me won't let me. His eyes look pained but strangely alert. He was afraid, but of what, the jocks from the football team? Maybe...

He shakes his head, smiling. "It's really nothing Anika. Don't worry about it. Oh, I have something for you." he says reaching into his backpack and pulling out my family's journal. Relief sweeps over me. I was starting to get anxious for it back. I wrap my hands around it carefully and cradle it in my arms.

"Thank you," I say,

"No, thank you. The book was quiet entertaining. I just can't bring myself to believe in all of the craziness. Thank you for the book though." He chuckles. Fury flares up inside me. After everything that's happened, he still won't see.

"Craziness? You're the crazy one! You refuse to open your eyes, to open your mind to the possibility just because it doesn't sound logical or real. You can't just expect everything to reveal itself to you. How do you think we managed to figure out everything we know now? We have to go off a hunch and see if it is real. You are blind to think just because you haven't seen one or it doesn't sound true means it's not real. That is no way to live. And it makes it harder to learn." I lecture him, but he just looks at me with laughter in his gold eyes which only makes my temper burst even more.

"Whoa! Sorry, I had no intention of offending you. Just in my personal opinion, it sounds like a scary story to keep children out of the woods so they won't get lost, kidnapped by cloaked strangers, or eaten by wolves." The image of the Dread that had been in my face a couple days earlier flashes in my mind. Fear and anger mix within me exploding, tears fill my eyes.

"You don't know anything. You're going to get yourself killed, and I'm going to feel responsible because I couldn't save you from your own stupidity. You know what, good luck. I hope you open your eyes soon. I don't want to find you dead. But it's up to you. Just… sigh, just be careful." I say turning on my heel and walking away quickly.

"Anika, wait! I still need to talk to you about it!" He calls but I don't stop, I run from the area as fast as I can so he can't see the tears. *Oh crap.* I think, *I do care about him.* I burst out the front doors of the school. I need to get away from it all, Xander, the Dreads, school, my family's birth right as monster hunters, everything. There is only one way to do that, escaping into a good book. Once I get home I shove my backpack in my room and keep my book with me. I head for the back door when my mom stops me.

"Where are you going missy?" She asks attempting to raise an eyebrow. My father and I can raise our eyebrows one at a time, but my mother can't; it was always strange to me that she couldn't, considering how easy it was for me.

"To my favorite spot to read, is that okay? If you call me on the emergency phone I'll come straight home, honest." I smile holding up my book. She thinks for a moment before she answers.

"All right, but come home as soon as I call. Don't be out too late, come home before dark if I don't call you earlier than that okay?"

"Thanks Mom! I love you!" I say as I hug her and disappear out the back door. I walk the path from the back door to the back gate and onto the path that was fifteen feet from the edge of the forest. No one ever walks the path except those assigned to watch it. That was either my father or the Darwins (Lani's family) who also hunt Dreads.

Lani's older brother Jackson, who is about nineteen, often accompanies his dad, my father and I on Dread hunts but lately they have decided on taking shifts. This month is their shift, next month is ours. It's a nice break every other month.

I follow the path to the hardest climbing tree along the edge of town. It has become my favorite one. When I was nine I conquered the tree, claiming it as my own, ever since then it's been my favorite reading spot. I sit down and open my book to the first page and begin to read. The story engulfs me immediately, taking me away from all of the annoyances of my life. I read pages and pages of it until I accidentally read myself to sleep…

~ ~ ~

I'm running for my life, trees flashing behind me. How did I even get into the forest? I wonder to myself trying to see the ground in ahead of me. I have a stressful feeling that I'm not moving fast enough. All I know is that I'm here and something is following me. I refuse to think of who or what it is. I run faster with all of my might, but no matter what I do, if it was cut corners or change direction, I can't lose it. To make matters worse, whatever is chasing me is gaining on me, and I'm getting tired. I start screaming for help, but my voice sounds raspy and weak like I have been yelling for a while now. I can hear the figure's foot steps right behind me. I know I'm not going to out run them; maybe I can fight them off. A strong hand grabs my shoulder and forcefully spins me around. I close my eyes and hold my breath as I'm pinned up against a tree, trapped. My hand reaches for my back pocket out of instinct for my dagger, but it's gone. I open my eyes in panic, only to find the most surprising thing in front of me. Xander is standing in front of me, watching me intently. What is he doing in the woods chasing me? "Anika… help." He whispers only to have a growl replace his voice. His grip on me lessens and he collapses to his knees, gasping. I'm frozen in place, unable to move or look away. He puts his head in his hands and screams. When he looks back at me his face has changed. His chiseled features are scaly, his gold eyes turn red and his teeth were fangs. What now stands in front of me is no handsome teenage boy, it's a Dread. It tilts its head when it looks at me, then launches itself at me, knocking me to the ground. It shrieks menacingly in my face baring its fangs, I scream…

    I bolt up, breathing heavily and feeling sweaty, with grass stuck to my arms and my head hits something hard. Like a rock or something, *but why would a rock be above me?* I rub my head and blink a couple times to get my vision to stop blurring. I also hear a deep male voice say, "Ouch," This brings me to full alert, I stand up and turn to run, but run into my favorite tree with so much force that I'm knocked down to the ground. I open my eyes to see Xander standing above me rubbing his forehead. Laughter is plain in his eyes and in his smile; he is trying so hard not to bust up laughing at my embarrassing little accident. "Anika, are you okay?" He chuckles holding out his hand to help me up. I push it away, and get up feeling a blush start on my face. I want to cry, or die from embarrassment. I've never lost my cool in front of anyone, and he is the last person I want to see what I just did. I brush off my jeans, my back towards him as I pick up my book. My legs are shaking like crazy. I feel like I'll fall over at any second. "Anika, come on. You look pretty frightened, what happened?" He chuckles. I turn to him, tears in my eyes. I blink trying to get rid of them.

"What do you want?" I growl.

"Me? I just saw you sleeping but it didn't seem pleasant or comfortable at all so I was going to wake you up, but it turns out I didn't need to. You sat up so quickly that we knocked heads." He shrugs, all laughter gone from his face.

"What are you doing on the path? People get attacked out here, it's not safe."

"What am *I* doing here alone? Anika, I'm not the young woman who should never be out alone, especially this close to dark, near the forest that people disappear in. Not to mention in this weather, it's about to rain."

"Don't you dare tell me what I can and cannot do. You don't know me; I am perfectly capable of taking care of myself. Why do you even care? All you do is embarrass me and make me feel stupid and foolish. Don't worry about me, you have no business to." I snap glairing.

"How dare I? How dare you Anika! I could say the same thing. You don't know me, and I can take care of myself. You tell me you don't want me to get hurt, but how in the world does that make sense? You insult me, yell at me, and roll your eyes at me as if I am inconveniencing you constantly. As if my existence bothers you. You can't tell me what to do, so stop trying to." He says, his voice calm, but his whole body rigid with anger.

"I know your type: over confident, high and mighty. They are always the ones who under estimate Dreads. They are the ones who get picked off first. Trust me; they can take you down effortlessly. I bet even I could take you down, easily." I say as I push past him, walking toward my house.

"You take me down?" he laughs,

"Oh, stop with your prideful male ego and go home." I say, rolling my eyes.

"There you go again, telling me what to do and rolling your eyes." Xander says running in front of me then turning and walking backwards so he can see me. I try to move past him but he blocks my path.

"Move," I say frustration, stopping in my tracks and folding my arms.

"Or you'll what?" He challenges, smirking making his dimples show. Anger rose inside me. I turn on my heel and walk straight to the forest. I hear his footsteps behind me, he grabs my arm, shudders went through me as images from my dream flash through my mind. "Anika, wait. Don't go through there." He pleads, I turn to look at him, his gold eyes were apologetic, his face pale. I smirk at this.

"Or you'll what?" I ask smugly. His face falls, and for a moment I feel bad for him. I must be confusing him a lot because he just doesn't seem to know what to do. That's when I realize it: he's in denial.

"Wait, why do you care whether or not I go into the forest?" I ask looking into his eyes, they avoid mine and he releases my arm. "You saw something didn't you? You're just in denial because you don't want it to be true. What did you see?" I push,

"Nothing, I didn't see anything. I don't know what you're talking about." He says stiffly, he's a horrible liar.

"Xander, I'm not stupid. I can tell you are in denial- and you are a horrible liar. Come on, what did you see?"

"I told you, I didn't see anything. Just a hooded figure in a cloak, but it wasn't clear and it doesn't prove anything. All I know is that people don't come back when they go in those woods." He says looking up into my eyes pleadingly.

"I do." I whisper. His eyes widen and he became interested. *Oh not again. Why can't I resist his charms?* I think.

"You go into the woods? Why?"

"Let's just say, I'm not as afraid of the Dreads as everyone else in town is. I do get freaked out when other people go into the woods without knowing what's waiting in it though." I smile a little.

"Aren't you afraid you'll get attacked?"

"No, I can protect myself. I'm not sure you can though. Curiosity could get you in a lot of trouble. You need to be careful Xander."

"I'm not scared though. I just need to figure it out."

"And you will, someday. Safely I hope."

"So you're not scared?"

"Not at the moment."

"Hmm, you are a mystery. I just don't get you."

"No one does." I smile in surprise at how much I could actually enjoy his company. He's still tense and keeps glancing at the forest. *Why is he acting so protective?* I wonder, but I figure that I should put him at ease so I walk back to the path. I feel so safe with him, I know he isn't afraid but he is at least cautious now. He's one of the only guys in Wolfsbane I can actually count on. But I also found it too easy to let my guard down when he's around me. That's when I again see flashes from my dream, I shudder.

"Are you cold? Here, take this." He says unzipping the blue hoodie he is wearing and puts it around me.

"Oh no, I couldn't possibly," I try to say but by that time his hoodie was around me and it's warm, so I decide it's best to just let him be chivalrous. I didn't realize how cold I really am. "Are you sure you won't freeze without it? It is about to rain you know." I state, and as if on queue, raindrops start falling from the sky. He smiles, showing his dimples, making me smile slightly, his cute smile was simply contagious.

"I'll survive. Besides it's getting late, we should head home. Hey, why don't you come and meet the rest of my family? I'm sure they would love to meet someone else from this town. No one has really made an effort to come get to know us. Only the cheerleaders have tried to get to know me but..." He pauses and thinks for a moment.

"I don't know," I reply.

"Please Anika, I'm begging you." He says giving me the cutest puppy dog eyes I had ever seen.

"Oh fine, just let me ask my mother."

"Okay," He smiles as I dial my house phone number.

~   ~   ~

We walk down the path a little ways until he turns to a huge, old, dark gray house. He opens the iron gate, and waits as I enter his back yard first. I take in a deep breathe as I look at the oldest house in Wolfsbane towering in front of me. A place I vowed never to enter when I was a child. The house is only one story tall but looks as if it had two because of its unusually large attic.

They have installed a basement into it which took longer then they had originally hoped. They had to get a contractor from out of town to install it because all contractors here don't dare to build around this home. They built the houses around it but had given this house quiet a bit of room. The yard is huge; their driveway is long, and house far from the road. The side yards on each side of the house are about the length of the house its self. Trees are all over the yard and the grass is long and no longer full of weeds. They planted flowers and put in a bench and a tire swing which makes it feel less forbidding.

The house even has its own legend. It's said to be first building built when the town was settled. The leaders built the house to be the town hall, where the town leader and his family would live, where leaders would meet and discuss things, and where the town would gather together for meetings. There were four families that founded Wolfsbane, Those families were the Brennus', the Darwins, the Dunstans, the Ulrics, and yes, my ancestors the Conalls. They came in from Scotland, Ireland and England, the explorers of their time.

They founded Wolfsbane and brought their families and friends over seas to start building the town. Clint Brennus was the leader. Charles Dunstan, Clint's assistant, documented the whole thing. Lani's ancestor, Edmund Darwin, Mangus Ulric, and my ancestor, Grant Conall were the guards of the explorers and close friends. Clint Brennus founded the small town and built the town hall. Clint moved in it as the town mayor. They brought down their families and several friends into the town, but dark things also came. Dreads appeared out of no where from the woods and killed Clint and his family in his home. Charles took his place and the Dunstans were in charge of the town for quiet some time.

Until Grant Conall, the one that wrote the journal about the Dreads, found out a terrible secret. The Dunstan's were half Dread. Charles wanted power so he used a curse that was passed through his bloodline to make himself unbelievably powerful. The people found out and where outraged and tried to execute him, but he and his family disappeared into the woods, never to be seen again. And now his descendents are far from human. They hunt down the town's people for food.

Soon the town looked to Grant to be the new leader but he declined saying his place was in protecting the town and its people, not leading them. They soon turned to Democratic solutions instead. No one went near the house after that and it's been empty until now. Some people say that Dreads have been seen looking through the windows of the house and figures and noises came from the house when it was supposed to be empty.

Xander follows me closely, watching me look at his rather large old house.

"You okay?" He asks.

"Fine, just fine," I say and give a brief explanation of the history of his home, my voice quivers as we walk through the back door of their home. He nods, half listening and closes the door behind us. The inside is totally remodeled. They have a huge kitchen and dinning room that is painted in a friendly yellow color. There is tons of space and it's surprising to me how different things were compared to the outside of the house.

"Mom, I'm home!" Xander calls. His mother pops up from behind the rather large island in the middle of the kitchen holding a tray of muffins. It surprises me so I jump right into Xander making me blush from embarrassment. His mother raises an eyebrow at her son who shrugs in return, both of them ignoring the fact that I can see what they were communicating.

"Who's this?" Mrs. Uriel asks as she studies me.

"Mother, this is Anika- a friend from my chemistry class."

"It's nice to meet you, Mrs. Uriel." I say holding out my hand, ready to shake hers.

"It's nice to finally meet you Anika." She replies smiling taking my hand, and pulling me into a hug.

I raise my eyebrow at the word finally and at the fact that she doesn't know me and was hugging me. *Where has she heard of me, and why a hug when a simple hand shakes would do?*

"Xander was right, you are very pretty. He always seems to talk about you for some reason. You seem to interest him. You are very different from other girls he has liked-"

"Mom, please. Not right now." He asks pleadingly. She smiles and then says "Anyone want a muffin? Just came out of the oven! They're blueberry Xander, your favorite!" He smiles and thanks his mother as he takes one for him and one for me. I'm surprised at how much they respect one another. Most boys in our town were rude to their mothers, but Xander is different. He walks right up to his mom and kisses her on the cheek.

"Where's dad? Is he home from work yet?"

"Oh yes dear. He is in the attic trying to figure out what was making noises up there last night." Then his mother went back to baking and we leave the kitchen.

"What noises?" I ask feeling a bit nervous.

"Yeah, probably a rat, or something. It's been making noises ever since we moved in. We still haven't found out what it is but my dad is setting traps for it. He explains as we enter the family living room. It would have been the town hall meeting room. It was very spacious. They had installed a fireplace and a couple of very nice looking couches. A beautiful grand piano and drum set were in one corner of the room. I eyed him suspiciously, smirking.

"Which do you play? Drums I'm guessing."

He shakes his head, "Why do you think you know everything about me? You honestly don't have a single clue." He smirks and walks on.

"So you play the piano?"

"Honestly, is it any of your business?" He laughs and goes into a hall way, I follow feeling foolish. *Why do I even care?* I wonder.

The hallway we enter is pretty long. There are four doors on each side and one door at the end of the hallway. As we pass the doors he tells me what each room is used for. The first door on the right is his little sister, Lucy's room. The second one is the library, the third his father's study the fourth is the bathroom. On the left side the first door is the master bedroom, then the guest room, then a closet, then another guest room. The door at the end of the hallway is the door that goes to the attic. When we approach the door the hallway seems to grow colder. Xander seems not to notice. He opens the door for me but I don't move.

"If you want, I can go first. The stairs are kind of scary to walk up." He offers, I nod in reply. He walks carefully up the creaky stair case; I follow closely at his heels. When we get to the top I see that the attic is huge and filled to the brim of really old things.

"None of the stuff in here is ours. The mayor wouldn't let us throw anything out so we just keep the door to it locked. No one likes coming up here, I hate it. It's creepy and old and smells like a public restroom sometimes…" Xander says disgusted. "Dad, you still up here?"

"Xander, my boy! You're home!" A deeper voice booms from the far corner of the attic. "Come here and look what I found. I need a trash bag as well, they are right by the stairs can you bring me one please?"

"Sure thing." He says as he grabs one. We head over to his father's voice. When his father looks at me he looks surprised.

"Who is this young lady? And why did you bring her in this nasty attic son?" He asks looking embarrassed.

"I'm Anika Conall, Xander's partner in chemistry class at school." I say holding out my hand waiting for him to shake it.

"It's nice to meet you, Anika. I would shake your hand but mine are kind of dirty. I've been cleaning up dead things out of here all afternoon." He says frowning.

"Dead things?" I ask realizing what the horrid smell was.

"Yep, Xander I don't think its rats making noise up here. This is why." He says reaching behind an old wooden dresser and lifting up a dead rabbit with a bite in it. I take a step back, so does Xander. "This is the third dead rabbit I've found today. And I've found several dead foxes as well. There is no way they can get up here on their own. And the bites in them are way too big to be rats."

I start to feel queasy. They have Dreads living in their attic and they don't even realize it. I look at Xander worriedly but he shakes his head. He's still in denial. His father drops the dead rabbit into the garbage bag Xander holds open. Then we all head down to the main level, His father locking the attic door behind us. I can tell his father and Xander feel uneasy. We walk from the hallway, I turn around to look at the door and the walls seem to close in around me. Underneath the door I see a shadow of feet behind it. Chills shudder through my body and I feel panic rise within me. Something is behind the door, standing. I put my hand on Xander's shoulder to steady myself. He turns to look at me, and I return his gaze then look back at the door, but the shadow is gone. *Had I imagined that?* I don't know.

We turn to the stairs that led to the basement. I follow him to a huge entertainment room. They have a large flat screen, a sectional couch, ping pong table and an air hockey table. I have a hunch that they were wealthy. It would cost tons of money to fix up this place, install electricity, and a basement and everything in it. Mason is sitting on the giant sectional watching football with Lucy sitting next to him grumbling.

"Can we watch something entertaining? Football is so boring! Why can't we watch 'My Little Pony," or 'SpongeBob' or something?" She whines.

"Hush, Lucy. I'm watching a game! Go Cowboys! Go! Go! Take it down field! Come on! Just pass the stinking ball!" Mason shouts at the television screen, his eyes practically glued to it. I see a Cowboys NFL flag and poster on the wall between the ping pong and air hockey tables. Obviously hard core football fans live in this home.

"Hey guys, I brought over a friend." Xander says looking at the television screen with interest. "Who is winning? What quarter is it?" he asks, entranced.

"It's the fourth quarter. Chargers are ahead by ten. We aren't doing so hot this year Xander." Mason answers, Xander shakes his head sadly. Lucy looks away from the screen and directly at me in surprise. I'm sure she doesn't think Xander would bring a friend that's a girl over. Her eyes widen and then she smiles. She walks over to me and introduces herself.

"I'm Lucy and I'm seven. Who are you?" She asks curiously

"My name is Anika. I'm in your brother's chemistry class." I say, still unsure if I should call Xander my friend. He sits down next to Mason watching the television screen closely. I shake my head, "Boys and their sports. I swear that's all they care about." I chuckle. Lucy nods and did something I don't expect. She walks right in front of the television and turns off the screen. I'm sure her brothers are going to freak out at her.

"Xander you have a guest! Stop watching this boring sport and hangout with her. It's rude to ignore someone you bring over." Her brothers look at each other in surprise.

"Alright Lucy, you're right. I'm sorry Anika, I got distracted." He says standing up from the couch. Mason just looks up at me and smiles, waving.

"Hello Anika. What a nice surprise to see you here. How are you doing?"

"I'm doing well thank you." I reply to him in surprise. I don't have any siblings but I've seen Lani battle over things like this with her brothers Jack and Kyle all the time. This family was very different from any family I have met before.

"Would you mind if I challenged you to a game of air hockey or ping pong?" Xander asks smiling.

"Why not, I'm up for a couple games."

I don't think Xander expected me to be good at either game. But I beat him at both every single time. I was trained to have fast reflexes and to react almost immediately after seeing something coming toward me. Mason and Lucy end up wanting to play against me. I let Lucy win, but I annihilate Mason.

"How in the world did you learn to do that? Your reflexes are amazingly fast." Mason asks. All I do in reply is shrug, but Xander looks at me suspiciously, he will not be fooled so easily.

~ ~ ~

His parents soon came down to join us, we talk they ask me about my family, the town, and about the animal attacks. I was very vague on each topic so eventually we just watch a movie, his mother picked it out. *'Pride and Prejudice'.* At the part at the ending when she meets Darcy in the meadow and they basically tell each other they love each other, both Mrs. Uriel and I tear up. Xander must have noticed because he seemed to feel uncomfortable. He reached over and patted my hand, then left his hand on top of mine. My hand felt hot and tingly under his, which was odd, I had never experienced this feeling before. Soon I felt my face get hot, *what was going on with me?*

A few minutes later, glass shatters, Darla starts barking, and then whimpering, things are falling over upstairs. We all jump, and Mason grabs the remote and pauses the movie. Xander's hand had grabs mine and he pulls me so I'm standing behind him. We all stare at the door that leads upstairs; no one moves at first, we only listen for more movement. There are no other sounds. One thing comes to my mind: Dreads are in the house. I feel vulnerable without my bow and arrows. Luckily I have my emergency dagger on me that my dad had given me when I was eight. It's tucked in under my jeans in a secret compartment that my mother had sown in every pair of jeans I own. They always wanted me to keep it on me. I felt myself reaching for it instinctively, but I stop myself. Both Xander and his father quietly walk toward the door to the upstairs. Mason and I follow their lead while Mrs. Uriel held Lucy close, clearly frightened.

    Xander turns to see me and shakes his head. 'Stay here.' He mouths, and then disappeared up the stairs behind his father and Mason. I ignore his orders and follow him up the stairs, his mother and Lucy close at my heels. They turn on the lights and walk to the kitchen entryway. A vase had shattered on the floor and chairs had fallen all over the place. Mr. Uriel walks around the kitchen slowly searching for something when he found their dog Darla under the table whimpering softly, looking terrified.

"Oh, Darla you silly girl. What's gotten into you lately?" He asked bending down and patting her head when he sees something that made him do a double take. "Lucy, get the first aid kit, Mason call the Vet, and Xander take Anika home, now." The whole family moves into action. I see what caused his alarm. Darla had a huge scratch on her back and it was deep and bleeding. I look down the hallway to see the attic door was slightly ajar, suddenly it closes. I feel like I'm in danger and all I want is for this sweet family to be safe. Xander leads me to the backyard as the rest of his family leaves the house for the vet. Except for Mason, who stays behind to clean up the mess. Xander lets me use his dark blue hoodie again and puts on a green one that made the green in his eyes pop. He insists on walking me home.

We walk in silence for a while, both of us unsure of what to say. Finally, I get up the courage to say something. "Xander, you and I both know what hurt Darla." I say slowly, watching my words carefully. He does not reply, he keeps his eyes on the ground and his hands in his pockets. "I know you don't want to believe they're real. But they are.

And that's something we all have to deal with," I continue. He stops walking; I stop too and watch him closely. He slowly looks up at me, his eyes hard with anger.

"I don't know what hurt Darla. But you still can't expect me to believe you. I know what you've said about them. I was spooked earlier today by a figure in the woods; maybe it was a person, maybe not. You still have no proof that Dreads are real." He says not moving, looking right into my eyes. A flash from my dream of a Dread covers his face, it startles me. I take a step back from him, breaking the connection of our eyes. He starts walking again and I follow, very slowly.

After a while he stops again and looks back at me with sad eyes. "Anika, I'm sorry about how you say I make you feel. I never mean to be rude or to embarrass you in anyway. I'm sorry that you don't like me very much and that we don't really agree easily. But I think I know why you treat me the way you do. You think I'm just some random jock that doesn't think of anyone other than myself and football. I hope you can give me the chance to prove you wrong. I'm stubborn, and it might drive you crazy, but I'm hoping you can look past the annoying things about me and that we can become good friends."

I just stare at him in shock. I had no idea that he wants to be good friends. I thought that he wanted us to get along because I have information on what happened to Victor. I had to process what he said in my mind to make sure I didn't mishear anything. That's when I hear one of the two sounds I dread the most.

"Xander! Xander is that you? What are you doing out here?" one shrill voice asks, the two girls giggle. *Oh great, Cheerleaders.* I think to myself trying not to roll my eyes. Xander turns as they approach, immediately turning on the charm, he smiles at them and I feel annoyed by his need for impressing everyone.

"Hello ladies, nice night for a walk isn't it?" I turn my head to see them as well; I know exactly who they would be. Nicki and Dana, but what are they doing out here so late this close to the forest?

No one but the Darwins, Conalls and now Xander walk the path in the whole town.

When both cheerleaders see me they look displeased. They circle around us like cats would after they trap mice. I hold my ground, I'm not about to cower in front of Nicki. I'm the only girl who doesn't care what she thinks. She will never boss me around. I would never let that happen. I've faced off with Dreads before, so she was easy to handle.

"What are you doing here?" She spits, folding her arms and glaring at me.

"Walking, what does it look like?" I answer simply.

"I meant with him." She snaps.

"Like I said before, we're just walking." I say folding my arms as well.

"Well, Bookworm. You're not welcome here, especially not with him." Dana spoke up, I want to laugh. *Since when was I not allowed on the back path? I'm one of the one's who guards it. And since when do they feel like they have power over me and can tell me what I can and cannot do?*

"Dana, I invited Anika on this walk with me. She's not intruding or anything, just leave her alone." Xander says in his charming deep voice. They ignore him to my surprise, they must really dislike me. Nicki only keeps studying me and Dana keeps blabbing on and on trying to insult me. I didn't pay attention, my focus is on Nicki. She looks me up and down as if she is sizing me up.

Was she going to try and fight me? Why? I haven't done anything wrong. Then I realize what I have supposedly done. I'm making her jealous because Xander invited me to go on a walk with him and hang out with him instead of asking her. She'd also repeatedly look at Xander's blue hoodie that I wore. She knows it isn't mine; it's too big for me. She has seen Xander wear it at school many times. Her face turns red with anger and her eyes staring daggers at me.

For some reason Dana stops talking and Nicki finally takes her eyes off me and looks over my shoulder behind me looking suddenly alarmed. I hear what has frightened them. Something snaps behind me in the forest. We all freeze staring into the forest trying to see what is moving inside it. It's too dark to see anything. I listen harder and hear leaves shuffling very quietly. Something is moving toward us. Then it went quiet, not making any sound. We all wait, listening for any sound, any movement that would give away location, but we hear none.

    I take a step back and bump into Xander, he sees that I'm nervous and grabs my hand which seems to calm me down for only a second, because right after he does, a Dread growls behind us, revealing its hiding place. We jump in fear and spin around to see the Dread grab Nicki and drag her into the forest kicking and screaming. Dana screams too in terror of seeing her leader getting pulled into the forest by a monster. I can only think of one thing and Xander says it.

    "Run!" He shouts and we all burst out into full sprints but all in different directions. Xander runs left, I ran right, and Dana of course follows

Xander's lead. I run hard and fast until my legs won't carry me anymore. But when I realize where I ran, I feel like an idiot. I ran right into the forest alone in the confusion. And I don't have my bow. I hear growling to my left, if no one saves me, I won't last the night.

I slow from a sprint into a jog, and then I just stop. I'm hopelessly lost. I didn't run in a straight line and I can't see anything so it's impossible to retrace my steps. I let out a frustrated sigh. I have to try to get out of here or I will die trying. I remember my copper dagger in my jeans. *Thank you mom and dad! They were right; you never know when you'll end up in a dangerous situation.* I think to myself as I bent down to unsheathe my dagger. Behind me I hear footsteps and freeze. I turn to look behind me and see blue cat's eyes reflecting in the dark. That normally wouldn't alarm me, except for the fact that they were directly at my eye level. I grip the copper dagger in my hand tightly. I turn to face the Dread only to be so horrified by what stands before me that I scream. The moonlight shows down into the forest revealing the most horrific thing my eyes have ever seen. The monster that stands before me was no ordinary Dread: It's Nicki.

~ ~ ~

Nicki is transforming into a Dread, half of her is still human, but the other half is anything but human. The left half of her body is covered in scale like skin. She still has her platinum blonde, shoulder length, straight hair and her red and black cheer sweats on. Her face is the most disturbing part. Half of it is scale like skin the other half is fair and flawless. She has a blue cat's eye on the side with the scale like skin and her normal human blue eye on the other side. Both different pupil shaped eyes glare at me full of hatred. The scales seem to be slowly spread across the rest of Nicki's face. I can't move; I can't believe my eyes. I don't understand why I'm so shocked by this. I knew that she must have look like this on the inside because of her personality. The thing that shocks me is that she is transforming into a Dread.

"Looking for a bite mark aren't you? Well there isn't one Bookworm. I was born this way; my father did an excellent job of hiding my secret didn't he? I can thank my mother for this, oh wait, no I can't- because you and your father killed her!" She snarls, all the sudden it hit me. Nicki's mother wasn't a Dread from what I remember, she was a strange woman who ended up disappearing into the woods one day and my father was sent to go look for her. We never found her, but we did kill a dread that day. But how was Nicki born like this? Wait, the story, Charles Dunstan's family line was cursed with the blood of the Dreaded; her mother came from the Dunstan line! But apparently Nicki developed camouflage like her mother. She looks human but is really a Dread. I never saw that coming, Dreads living amongst the towns people.

"Well, well Bookworm. Look at the mess you've made for yourself. The question is why? Why did you have to deny me my right as a leader? Why are you trying and take Xander from me? Why must you rebel against my rules?" she asks smirking, showing me her menacing looking retractable fangs.

"You being Mayor Rune's daughter does not give you power over anyone else. You don't scare me." I reply keeping my voice steady and trying to breathe deeply and slow down my heart beat. She laughs at my words; I know she can smell my fear and hear my heart that's pounding a million beats a second.

"You have no idea how long I've been waiting for a moment like this: to catch and trap you in the woods all alone. No one can save you, and you don't have that stupid bow. I never thought I'd see the day! And yet here we stand, as if fate wants me to show you how much I truly hate you and your pathetic little family." She lunges at me and I dodge her attack swinging my dagger at her but she sees it and knocks it out of my hand with such force my wrist brakes. I yell out in pain as she grabs my injured wrist and begins to twist my arm, attempting to break it. Luckily my father taught me hand to hand combat. I kick her in the stomach and she releases me but cuts my shoulder with her talons. Warm blood trickles down my arm and back and soak the ripped sleeve of my shirt and Xander's blue hoodie. I turn and run as fast as I can. I have to get away or she will kill me.

"I'm not finished with you yet!" Nicki snarls, the smell of my blood driving her into frenzy, she runs after me.

When she catches up to me again she slams me into a tree, knocking all the oxygen out of my lungs. I now lie helplessly on the ground gasping for air, holding my bleeding shoulder and feeling tears stinging my eyes. Despite my adrenaline rush, my body aches and I'm starting to feel faint and slow due to the paralyzing poison in her talons. That and I'm losing a lot of blood. I stumble as I try to get up and feel so dizzy that I almost pass out, but my adrenaline refuses to let me. Nicki pins me against a tree with her claws, my vision is starting to blur. I try to struggle to get away but I can feel my strength vanishing. I spit in her eye and then became a dead weight. She jumps back when I spat at her and growls at me letting me slump to the ground. She uses her claws to cut open my side as I try to crawl away. I groan and she throws me against two more trees before I stop moving. I know I can't fight her anymore.

Chapter 8: Rescue

-Xander

I sprint for my life with Dana right beside me. I look over my shoulder to make sure Anika is right behind me, she's no where to be seen. I come to a dead stop and look around frantically. Panic rises inside me, "Where's Anika?" I demand. Dana gives me an answer when she turns to look back at the forest in terror. "Are you serious? Did you see her go in there?" Dana didn't even have to answer. A scream comes from the woods, a different one than Nicki's. I know it has to be Anika's. "We need to get help now!" I say pulling out my iphone and dialing Mason's phone number. Mason answers after the second ring.

"Xander, what's up?"

"I need your help. Get a bunch of people together that are brave enough to go into the woods. Bring some sort of weapons and flash lights ASAP, got it?" I say turning to the forest and walking in the direction of my house.

"What's going on Xander? Did something bad happen?" Mason asks seriously. I take a deep breath.

"There was an attack. Nicki and Anika got dragged into the woods by… something. I don't think Nicki is okay but I heard growling and Anika was screaming."

"On my way now, I'll bring friends." He replies, and then hangs up the phone.

Mason gets here faster than I thought he would. It only took him about ten minutes to gather up several teens, flashlights, baseball bats and butcher's knives. Among the teens were Kyle, his sister Lani, Anika's friend Melanie and some boys from the football team: Marcus, Brad, Kaleb, and Andrew. Mason ran up to me, handing me a bat and a flashlight.

"I told them about Nicki and Anika and they rushed right over. I called the authorities and they said to hang tight and wait for them, they'll be over here soon." He says looking worried.

"Not soon enough," I think about Victor's body. "Look, when the police will get here, it will be too late to save them. Either we go in and find them, or leave them to die. I am going in. Who ever wants to save them will follow me. If you don't want to no one is forcing you. It's your choice." I say and everyone nods. "Girls, you'll stay here and tell the authorities what is going on and watch to see if Anika or Nicki finds their way out of the forest. The rest of you guys, follow me." I say, my tone meaning business. I turn and hurry toward the forest, chills creep through me as I cross the line into the forest.

We don't hear anymore screams. We move quickly, calling their names and listening intently. This happens for a while as we move deeper and deeper into the forest. It's dark, you couldn't really see anything that the moon's light silhouettes or the flashlight's light didn't show you. Soon we hear something freaky: laughter- cruel, insane, scary laughter. We all think the same thing and turn off our flashlights as we move in on the sound. We creep slowly and stealth like, trying to blend with the forest. Eventually one figure that is standing came into view, it seems to be looking down at something, and the moon light revealed a second figure lying still covered in dark liquid. I can't stand it anymore. I turn on my flashlight and point it directly at the two figures. The standing one turns around and to my horror and disbelief I realize what it is.

    A Dread, a real live Dread stood there, watching me. It looks just like the picture in the book Anika showed me; the only difference was that it had platinum blond hair. It stares into my soul with its piercing blue eyes and hisses. I take a few steps back until I see the figure on the ground. A girl with long brown hair that's wearing my dark blue hoodie lies on the ground unmoving, lifelessly still. The hoodie is soiled in blood.

    "Anika!" I yell, taking immediate action, my group follows my lead. I run toward the hideous creature, my baseball bat is ready to take a hard swing at it. The creature disappears from my view within seconds. Next thing I know it's attacking my brother. He punches and kicks at it, squirming to escape the monster's grasp but nothing he does phases the beast. It sinks its claws into his skin causing him to yell out in pain. I come to my brother's rescue only to be pushed forcefully into a near by tree. Kyle tackles the beast to the ground off of Mason.

"Get off of my friend you monster!" Kyle shouts trying to pin the Dread down. Kyle was the only one of us who brought a knife with him. He stabs the Dread in its shoulder. The beast growls in pain, the color of the knife was strange. I realize it was Copper. The Dread bit Kyle's neck and his body fell limp. The monster pushes him off and went for the football jocks. I approach Kyle carefully and turn him over. His eyes were white and filmy. Then his body starts to shake as if he is having a seizer. I yell for help and Mason joins my side. *I'm scared out of my mind. What am I supposed to do?*

"Mason, stay with him. I need to get Anika out of here." I say, he nods. I run over to her, only to be blocked by the Dread. It pins me against a tree so fast I don't realize what happened until I felt something against my back. It stares at me, looking deep into my eyes. There is something familiar about them. Next thing I know, the creature vanishes into the dark. We wait for a few minutes to get attacked again but it never came. I get to Anika and pick her up carefully. I hear faint breaths and her heart is still beating. Thankfully she's still alive. She looks almost as bad as Kyle does and she's unconscious but alive. I hold her in my arms and think about how lucky I had gotten. *Why didn't the Dread harm me?* I think to myself.

Kyle's seizer stops but he seems as if he's dead. We search for a pulse but find none. The rest of the guys help carry his body out of the forest and back to town where paramedics, police men, and the whole town wait for us. *This is going to suck.* I sigh as the Paramedics take Anika from my arms and place her onto a gurney, Kyle is also placed on a gurney and his ambulance takes off immediately. The others and I are loaded into one ambulance and ride in silence to the town hospital. My brother is bleeding from several deep cuts and after examining me they told me I have a concussion.

At the hospital we are all taken into one giant room where they could fit eight patients at a time. Mason and I are placed on beds near each other. The doctors examine us quickly. I have cracked a rib on my left side which was why it was hurting and I have a mild concussion. They say I should take things slow for a couple days and that with my broken rib I shouldn't play football this season. They sentence me to a week in the hospital. Mason is stitched up and sent home, as were most of the football players. All of them except for Kaleb, a poor guy that has a broken leg that is bent at an angle that it should never go. He is also out of the rest of the season this year.

Chief of Police of Wolfsbane Chief Darwin, Kyle's father, and the town's Deputy is Anika's father, come to interview me. They take me in a meeting room, close the door and the blinds. The room has blue walls, white tiled floors, a metal table, and three metal chairs, two by the door side of the table, and one on the wall side. I feel very small in this room.

"Sit." Chief Darwin commands in a deep bass voice that sends shivers down my spine. I can tell I'm in a lot of trouble, I obey without hesitation. Neither officer sits down, Deputy Conall paces the floor but Chief Darwin stands in front of me quietly, deep in thought. Probably trying to pick what words he needs to say. I wait, not daring to interrupt his thoughts. Then he finally sits down across from me and looks into my eyes. "What happened out there?" he demands seriously. This question startles me; I wasn't sure what to say. That's when I realize that I'm in shock, everything was a blur and nothing felt real. I open my mouth to speak but no words come out. "I know this is hard for you. You saw a lot of things you wish you hadn't, but please, tell me what happened." The chief asks again, patience in his voice.

"I was walking Anika home when we ran into some kids from school,"

"What kids?" Deputy Conall interrupts in mid pace.

"Nicki Rune and Dana Crowley." I answer wondering why it matters. Deputy Conall and Chief Darwin look at one another with weary eyes.

"Then what happened?" Chief Darwin presses,

"The girls started arguing and I tried to get them to stop. Then we heard a snapping sound. Next thing I knew, Nicki was being dragged into the forest by some… thing and we all ran. Anika ended up in the forest somehow and I went after her. Some of the football guys, my brother, and Kyle went with me. We found Anika but were attacked by whatever had dragged Nicki into the forest. Everything else is a blur." I say honestly, feeling more and more exhausted by the minute. The two officers look at each other with sad eyes. They each have a child that has gotten hurt- and they were both hurt because of me.

I put my head in my hands. This whole thing is my fault. If I left Anika alone, she would have gone home and no one would have gotten hurt. I feel numb inside and unsure of what to do. I miss California, where nothing like this would ever happen. But here I am and I have to face the facts. Two friends- no, two families were hurt and the whole town is scared out of their minds because of me. I feel a hand on my shoulder and look up. To my surprise, it's Chief Darwin. He looks down at me with sympathetic eyes.

"Listen kid, this whole thing isn't your fault okay. It was a horrible accident. They attacked you. You're lucky that you guys are still alive. You are a hero- If you got their any later Anika would have died due to blood loss. You chose to save her and got there right in time. I'm sorry you had to see those things. Next time, just call us and we will get there as soon as possible, okay?" The chief says quietly. I nod slowly as the chief walks to the door. "You may go back to your hospital room, you look exhausted, I'll go get a nurse." He says opening the door and exiting the room. Deputy Conall stays in the room; I stand and walk over to the door to leave when he stops me.

"Thank you, for saving my daughter. Not many people would have risked that for her. You are a good friend that she's lucky to have." He says honestly to me. I can't look at him, I feel ashamed. His daughter is hurt and there is still a chance that she might not make it. I keep my eyes on the ground. He pats me on the back and we leave the room, he closes the door behind him.

~ ~ ~

After a week, they finally release me from my prison of a hospital room and let me see my family.

"Hey bro, how are you doing?" Mason asks as I approach. My mother opens her arms and hugs me. I hug her back and reply, "Fine." Both Mason and my dad look nervous. There was something they aren't telling me.

"What is it?" I demand. My whole family looks at each other, unsure of what to say. "Tell me." I demand more forcefully. My mother's eyes are now wet with tears. Mason clears his throat getting emotional as well, and Lucy starts to cry.

"Kyle and Anika are in Acoma. Kyle has been poisoned by that strange animal bite. He's dying slowly; there is nothing they can do. That's not all," He says, looking at the floor and rubbing the stitches on his hurt arm. My mother takes his hands in hers and hugs him. I look at my father questioningly.

"Xander," He says, looking uncomfortable. I wait, letting him choose his words. He sighs and just goes right out to say it. "Xander, Darla is gone. She was infected with a similar poison that they can't cure. They ended up just putting her down so she wouldn't be miserable anymore. I'm sorry son. I know how much you cared for her. You practically trained and raised her all by yourself. But she's in a better place now," He says awkwardly. My father has never handled death well, he hates talking about it. I don't handle it well either. I turn on my heel and walk away from them. I need to clear my head, that's when a nurse found me wandering.

"Mr. Uriel, Ms. Conall is asking for you. Follow me; I'll take you to her room."

I follow her quietly down the hallway to room A45. The window to the room was open and Anika lay in the bed, looking at today's paper. I pause in front of the door, feeling suddenly nervous, yet relieved. She was going to be okay. I turn the knob and open the door, it creaks making Anika look up from the paper. She smiles, which surprises me. I thought she'd be angry with me. After all, the whole thing is my fault.

"Well if it isn't my 'Knight in Shining Armor'," She says teasingly.

"Yeah right, if I were your knight in shining armor you wouldn't be in the hospital right now, and you wouldn't have almost bled to death." I say sitting in the metal fold up chair next to her bed.

"Don't you dare blame yourself for that. If it weren't for you I would've died in those woods. I'm the one that ran into the forest like an idiot and made enemies with the wrong people," she tries to explain, and then her eyes suddenly grow dark as if she was remembering something unpleasant.

"Is something wrong?" I ask, looking into her eyes with concern, she shakes her head as to rid the memory from her thoughts and looks down at the paper.

"So, I hear you're the town hero now?" she says picking up the town paper, The Wolfsbane Journal, and shows me the article. "We even made the front page," She tries to laugh, the headline read: "Pretty Boy Saves Local Girl." Below it is a picture of me carrying Anika out of the forest. I push the paper aside and take a deep breath.

"I only wish I had gotten to you sooner." I say, and it was followed by an awkward silence between us.

"Oh, I almost forgot." She says and turns to pick something up. She whimpers and holds her side in pain as she comes back with my dark blue hoodie in her hand. It had been washed but it's stained with her blood and has several rips in the fabric that were sown together, one on the shoulder, another and a long one on the side. She hands it to me with an apologetic look on her face. "I'm sorry about the stains. My mom tried her best to wash them out…" She says, looking embarrassed.

"It's no worry. You're alive and that's all that matters." I say accepting my hoodie from her. She releases it and lies back on the bed looking exhausted.

"Thank you, you know- for saving my life." She says as the door behind me opens.

"Any time," I chuckle and turn around to see her father entering the room. I stand up and leave so they can be together. Today is the day they were finally letting me go home, and I have a dog, my best friend, to bury...

~   ~   ~

There are only a couple of times you will ever see a young man cry. For me, this is one of those times. I walk into the woods near the corn fields and dig a pit big enough for Darla. She was a Pointer-Labrador dog and she had only been five years old. To make it worse, today is her birthday. She was going to turn six, a canine in her prime. I let the tears fall freely and don't wipe them off. It hurt too much, all of it: losing my dog, Kyle lying in a hospital waiting to die, almost losing

Anika, moving from my home in California to come to this nightmare of a town.

I keep digging until my cracked rib can't take it anymore. I throw the shovel on the ground angrily and yell until my voice is raspy and aches. I don't care if those monsters came; I dare them to come after me. I fall to my knees, anger, sadness, and confusion run through me. *Why did this have to happen?* I think angrily, crying again. I take five minutes to recompose myself then I continue digging.

Soon the pit is finished; I set her down carefully in it and toss a few flowers I had bought earlier. After I finish filling the grave, I carve a heart and a 'DU' in the middle of the nearest tree to where I buried her, then I sit down next to the grave for a while, thinking. When the sun starts to set I figure that I should head home. I decide to take a short cut through the corn fields. The sunset creates an orange glow on the clouds. I take one last look at the woods before emerging into the corn fields. I move with ease through the corn stocks, composing myself with every step. I know I'd be able to get through it in time. The walk through the field seems endless, even though it has only been about few minutes. I'm not far from the edge when I hear a noise behind me, I freeze in place. I wait for another sound and when I hear none I continue walking when I hear a second noise. I flip around and something I see startles me.

Nicki is standing behind me a few yards away smiling flirtatiously. I take a step back in shock, I can't believe my eyes. She has been missing for a week and no one could find her after the accident. But here she is, standing in front of me as if nothing had happened. "Oh Xander, I've missed you." She says mischievously, circling me slowly. I feel threatened, something about her is off. The way she looks at me is like I am something to eat. As if I'm a sheep and she's a wolf who has been stocking and observing me from afar for too long. "So, did you miss me? Did you wonder where I went or what happened to me?" She asks stopping in front of me now. "Or did you brush it off? Forget about me, say that I was fine or that I had died and it was a lost cause to look for me?" she says angrily now, facing away from me.

"Nicki, I was very concerned about you. But I found Anika and she was being attacked by a monster, I had to save her and make sure she'd live." I try to explain, she tenses up at my words.

"Monster? So I'm a monster now!" She screams, turning toward me suddenly. Her eyes are like a cat's now, her finger nails grow into claws, and she seems to be more muscular and slightly taller than before, that's when I recognize the eyes-the same eyes of the monster that pinned me to the tree on the night of the attack only a week earlier. She growls at me and tackles me to the ground with strong force, so fast I thought I imagined it. I yell in surprise and try to push her off of me, but she ended up sinking her fangs and teeth into my forearm instead. I yell out in pain and kick her in the chest, knocking the wind out of her. She slides off me, coughing up my blood and gasping for breath. I crawl away and stand up, then sprint as fast as my legs can carry me away from the corn field. I need to get home, or around people. "Xander! Come back you coward!" She screams not far behind me, her voice more monstrous than before.

I find myself out of the corn field and onto the football field. I don't stop running until I reach my front door. I lock it and hurry dizzily to my room after grabbing the first aid kit from the kitchen. I look at the bite in my forearm, it's gruesome and blood is gushing out of it. I clean the wound quickly and wrap it in gauze. After that I stand up to put away the first aid kit when the room begins to sway, my wound, lungs, and veins start to burn with scorching fire and my heart aches and I can't breathe. Soon I notice my floor seems to be getting closer until everything goes black.

Chapter 9: Transformation
-Anika

I watch Xander leave the room and smile at my father when he sits down in the chair next to my hospital bed. "Hey, how are you feeling?" My father asks me grabbing my hand looking very concerned.

"Better, surprisingly. Even the doctors don't understand how I'm still alive and why I'm healing so fast. It does hurt a little, but not as much as it should. I mean, in the forest I was thrown against trees... I should have broken something," my father smiles to himself deep in thought. I wonder what is on his mind but he doesn't tell me.

"Have you heard any news on my other friends?" I ask looking at my hands. The feeling in my stomach is uneasy. I hope that the feeling doesn't mean anything. My father doesn't respond for a while, I hold my breath. *Something is wrong. Someone's hurt.* I'm not sure how I know, I just do. I can sense it somehow. I know someone in this hospital is hurting badly, and they feel familiar. I look back at my father with worried eyes. "Who's hurt? What happened?" I demand. My father sighs; he is never good with emotional things. He hesitates, unsure of how to start.

"Kyle was bitten." He says suddenly. I can't breathe, I feel as if I were just punched in the gut.

"He was *bitten*?" I whisper in shock wanting it to be a cruel joke, but the look on my father's face is serious. He's telling the truth. I feel hollow inside, it can't be true. I know my father would never lie to me but I still do not want to believe him. "I need to see him." I say seriously. I struggle getting off the sheets and trying to turn my body to get off the bed. The deep dull pain is awful and makes my movements jagged, stiff, and robotic. I'm slow but I eventually swing my legs over the edge of the bed. To my surprise, my father has not tried to stop me. He watches me with interest. I slowly, carefully, put my left foot on the floor followed by my right. The tile is ice cold and smooth against my feet.

I gather all of my strength and attempt to stand. I'm rewarded by falling face first on the floor and tangling myself in the IV tubes. My father still only watches intently, not moving even now that I'm sprawled out on the floor. I grunt as my muscles scream; my legs have given out on me. I gather my all my will power and push myself off the ground, ripping out my IV tubes in annoyance. Next thing I know, I'm standing, limping dizzily out of my room with my father following at my heels. I limp down the hallway watching what the doctors and nurses are doing. They all seem to be rushing towards one particular area of the Hospital. I know that was where Kyle is.

The Emergency Room is buzzing with people; no one looks at me once. They are all rushing, too busy with their jobs to bother with me. The Emergency Room is never full and neither is the hospital. Everyone in Wolfsbane is pretty healthy. We don't really care for contact with the outside world so the Mayor built us a small hospital. It's the same size as the High School. There were about twenty people who work here, the hospital doubles as our Doctor's Office as well. They normally aren't very busy, they mostly fix broken bones, help people with diabetes, colds, viruses, and deliver babies but those things rarely happen here. Never once have they ever actually caught someone who has been bitten by a Dread before the person died. It's the most exciting thing that has happened in town. I wonder how they are trying to help Kyle survive. We know nothing of the Dread venom except for how it paralyses you for about an hour.

I see Lani's family sitting next to the windows and doors of the Emergency Room peering through the windows anxiously. I stand beside Lani and put my arm around her shoulder, both to comfort her and balance me. She looks at me, she has bags under her eyes and her skin is pale and splotchy. She looks like she hasn't slept in days and has been crying a lot. She hugs me and I hug her back, not saying a word. There are no words that I can say to comfort her or her family. Our families are the only ones who know how bad a bite from a Dread really is. Kyle is going to die from it.

After a long hug, I look over at her parents and her older brother Jackson. They all look like they haven't moved from this spot in days. It's as if they are all half dead. My father goes and stands by Chief Darwin whispering quietly to him. I only catch a few words. "Stronger than I thought… earlier than expected… need to be ready." I wonder what they are talking about and why they are looking at me and Lani when they say it. I turn to the window and decide to just brush it off. I look in the window unsure of what to look at. All I can see was the blinds that are closed in front of it. I can see little of what is going on through the cracks but it isn't very clear. The doctors look busy at work, but I'm not sure what they are doing. No one knows how to cure a Dread bite. When I try to see more Lani finally speaks.

"You don't want to see it. It's horrifying." She says numbly. Putting her head against the glass and beginning to cry silent tears. Jackson comes up to me and puts his hand on my shoulder.

"If you really want to see, I will take you. I can't stand here and wait for nothing to happen forever. I will go crazy if I do." He looks at me sadly and I follow his tall, lean figure down the hallway a little ways. I have always been close with their family. Ever since I was a little kid. I feel like we are really just one big family. Sure the Darwin kids were all older than I am, Kyle is the youngest in their family but he was only born a few weeks before me. I feel connected to them somehow. They all are pretty tall, well except for Lani who is an inch shorter than I am but always makes up for it by wearing high heels. The whole family has blonde hair and hazel or brown eyes and olive toned skin. They are always together; they are the closest family I have ever known. It's heartbreaking that Kyle is dying.

    We turn a corner and Jackson stops in front of a window, waiting for me to catch up to him. He flips his long hair out of his face, his eyes shadowed and empty looking. He turns to the window and stares at the scene playing out before him. I look into the room when I reach the window only to be horrified at what I see. Kyle is tied down to a metal table in the middle of the room as doctors and nurses extract blood, spit, sweat, and skin samples. He lies very still with his eyes closed, his skin is a sickly yellow color and he has a wet sheen on his face, arms, and legs as if he is sweating like crazy. The bite in his neck must be deep because it is still bleeding. A nurse goes over to him with a new bandage, about to replace the bloody bandage on his neck. When she removes it I almost scream, I have to cover my mouth to block it. The wound in his neck is deep serrated and the skin around it is turning scale like and seems to be spreading from there.

No, no, no! This can't happen! He can't be turning. Not into one of them. I scream in my mind, silent tears fall from my face. Jackson says nothing, only watches the nurse replace the bandage. As soon as the bandage touches the skin on his neck, Kyle begins to shake as if he is having a seizer. The nurse calls out for help, his arms flail about and an unmistakable growl fills the hospital, it comes from Kyle's mouth. His arms suddenly become tight and strained and his eyes shoot open, they are completely black. He pushes the nurse with such force that she hits the wall near us. There is shouting as doctors rush to hold him down but it's no use, he busts the metal bonds that hold him to the table and shoves the doctors this way and that. When he roars again he has fangs. He leaps off the table and crashes through a wall that happens to be right next to the window Jackson and I are watching the chaos unfold. Jackson grabs me and pulls me back so fast I don't know what's happened.

And there Kyle stands in front of us, glaring, growling and angry. He's huge and looks too much like a Dread. The only way I know it's Kyle is his blonde hair and his facial features; all that is left was the scale-like skin which is spreading quickly from his bite wound. Jackson stands in front of me protectively; I think he has finally lost it.

"Kyle, I know you're still in there. You have to fight it. I know it's hard but you are one of the few that can. Please, don't let it take control of you. You're too strong for that." Jackson states seriously, and takes a step forward. Kyle shakes his head and opens his eyes again and they are brown. He looks at his hands and his eyes widen. The scales on his hand told him one thing, he is turning.

"Guys, what's going on?" Kyle asks fear plain in his voice. He stares at the scale-like skin that covers his arms. Fearful he looks up at us, the brown in his eyes being consumed by the black of his pupils. Then charges past us and breaks through another wall, escaping into the outside world. Jackson and I run toward the wall only to see Kyle disappear into the forest. Just like that my friend, my brother, had died and been replaced by a monster.

~ ~ ~

That night they sent me home seeing that I am well enough to walk around and they shut down the hospital because it is in need of extensive repairs and it is too dangerous to stay inside the building. The news of Kyle's transformation travels fast across town. The fear that stuck with the story takes over like a deadly virus. My father and Chief Darwin suggest that we have a new curfew that the Mayor reinforced. Mayor Rune tries to gather a search party to find Kyle and Nicki. Only my father and Chief Darwin volunteer which is no surprise. My mother takes me home and helps me to my room. We both know that this will be a hard transition. Things are changing and they are changing way too fast.

I lie in my bed and stare at the ceiling. There is no way I'm going to be able to sleep tonight. I look over at the clock at my nightstand. It informs me that it is one in the morning. On the bright side, it's now a Saturday. My mind keeps wandering to Kyle, I wonder if he is okay and if there is a possible way we can save him. I groan as I lift myself out of bed. I walk down the hallway and into my dad's study, searching for books and ways to find a possible cure. I search for hours until I end up falling asleep on the arm chair down there. Much to my disappointment, I found nothing that resembles or even mentions a cure.

When I wake up the next morning I'm in my bed. The smell of French toast with strawberries and cream wafts through the air, a treat like this is rare in this house. We normally have a fruit and veggie smoothie and Bran cereal for breakfast. I will myself to my feet and dress out of my pajamas and get dressed for the day quickly. When I arrive in the kitchen I stop cold in my footsteps. Mayor Rune is there at the table sitting in front of a plate of freshly made French toast. He turns to look at me and an instant flash of Nicki's true form appears in my mind. I only stare at him. "Ah, Ms. Conall, finally awake I see. It's good to see you so well and healed. That week in the hospital must have been hard on you. It's amazing to see what a quick recovery you had. It still boggles the doctor's minds." He says, his deep dark eyes peer into mine. He looks suspicious of me; I don't know why he would. I'm just as confused and amazed about my recovery as he is. We watch each other closely, I'm not thrilled about his presence in my house and he is clearly not happy to be here. Probably because I'm still here and his now monster of a daughter is gone off in the woods somewhere. I walk slowly to the other side of the table, not taking my eyes off him.

I take my seat and my mother places a plate in front of me. She smiles and looks happy to see that I'm back and that I am safe and sound. She has piled my plate with French toast. She gives me a small quick hug before returning to the stove to cook some eggs. My mother seems terrified for some reason; I notice she won't look the Mayor's direction. I wonder what they had been speaking about before I came in. He watches me eat my food, not even touching his plate or fork. It's unsettling. To my surprise I finish all of the French toast on my plate and am still hungry. "So, what brings you to this side of town?" I ask trying to hide the dislike that coats my voice, it doesn't work.

"You do Ms. Conall." He says simply, a smirk settles on his features. The Mayor is about forty years old. His skin is paler than any person I have ever seen, he has his long black hair pulled back in a stupid ponytail and cold dark eyes just like his daughter even though Nicki's eye are blue instead of black. He is tall and thin and always has a smug look on his face as if he knows something you don't. His nose is pointed and cheek bones are so high and gaunt it looks unnatural. Sometimes I wonder how in the world he was voted to represent our town as the leader and then I remember that he uses his silver tongue to convince the people for votes along with his financial influence. My father strongly disagrees with him at almost every turn. He does nothing for the community and seems to have secret agendas of his own. Some people respect him, most fear him. The only ones who don't are my father, Chief Darwin, Jackson and myself. I finally speak knowing if we are going to have a stare down it would last forever.

"What do you want from me?" I keep my tone even. He stands from his chair and slides the plate full of French toast aside replacing it with a brief case.

"I want to know what happened to my daughter. I know you were the last to see her. I want to know where she went." He says looking at me calmly. He is too calm, he knows where she is, and wants to know if I know. He has come to me because he knows I can't lie very well. I'm not sure how but he seems to know what everyone's weaknesses in town are.

"She disappeared into the woods, a Dread took her. But I'm sure she is very much alive. I don't know where she is. I assume in the forest somewhere." I reply casually, shoveling some eggs into my mouth that my mom has served up. Mayor Rune clearly knows I'm not going to say anything else, but he knows I'm not telling the whole story. His eyes narrow at me.

"How did you get out of the forest alive? No one that goes in ever comes out alive. How did you manage to?" He asks rather forcefully, I am surprised that he has not read the paper which has all of that information on it.

"I was rescued by a friend, a couple of friends actually."

He watches me for a while, thinking. Then he unlocks his brief case and pulls something out of it and sets it on the table. I then realize it is two copper daggers he has pulled out. I recognize my own dagger immediately, but the second one I have never seen before. Both have family code of arms imbedded on the steel hilt. The seal on my dagger has a wolf in the center and two arrows making an 'X' behind it. The other dagger has five battle axes and a plus sign in the back ground imbedded in the hilt. I have seen it once before. It is the Darwin's code of arms. The dagger is Kyle's.

"Where did you get those?" I demand, standing up in my chair, glairing at him.

"You should really keep better track of your belongings Ms. Conall, sometimes when you loose something, it doesn't always come back." He says snapping his brief case and turning to leave as quickly and mysteriously as he came. I only watch him go having the sudden urge that I want to tear him limb from limb. I'm not sure what makes me feel that violent inside, but it is strong. My mother closes the door behind him after he wishes us a good day, but he seems know has already spoiled it.

Chapter 10: Hybrid
-Xander

My eyes fly open and I begin to gasp for air. My body stings and aches everywhere. I want to scream but nothing comes. I stare hopelessly at my ceiling trying to move. I notice that I'm sweaty and sticky. My whole body and all of my clothes are drenched in my own sweat. It's as if I jumped into a lake and then lay down on my floor, even the carpet is wet. Once I push back the terror of wondering what is happening to me I realize that I need to get up. I take deep breaths as I concentrate on trying to move some part of my body. I feel my fingers twitch, that's a good sign. I suddenly feel very thirsty and starving. I need food badly, at this thought my body suddenly responds to me. I slowly push myself up with my arms only to be greeted by a painful stabbing feeling in my forearm. I collapse once again, grunting. I look at my arm and see the bandage I put on it and remember what had happened. The gauze is now soaked with my blood. The bite feels like it is on fire, so did my heart and lungs.

I again try to get up, my empty stomach consumes my thoughts and I ignore the pain. Once I stand I feel dizzy again, but not as dizzy as before. Something about me feels different; I look at my arms again to see that they are more defined and muscular. I touch by side with the cracked rib, it used to hurt when I place pressure on it but now I feel no pain. *That's strange, seriously what is going on?* I take my first few steps and stumble into my dresser, breaking it. *Oops… Mom is going to kill me for that.* Soon I finally get to my bedroom door which has a mirror hanging from it. I reach for the door knob when I think I see something crazy. I look right into the mirror and freeze. There staring back at me is me- well a version of me that has bright hazel cat's eyes. I yell in surprise and when I open my mouth I realize that I have long, sharp, pointed, white retractable fangs. *What's happening to me?* I throw open the door and grab a hoodie and some sun glasses. I run upstairs to the kitchen and open the fridge. I rummage around looking for anything that looks good enough to eat. I then catch a whiff of something that smells irresistible, but it isn't coming from the fridge. I spin around to see Lucy standing a few feet away from me looking concerned. I realize it was her that smelled good enough to eat. Terror swells through me as I realize what I'm thinking. I turn back around and hold my breath. Maybe I'm going insane, I 'm not sure what is going on but I have to get out of here.

"I heard you scream downstairs, is everything okay? What's with the sun glasses? It's raining outside you know." My sister says curiously, I ignore her and grab anything that looks appealing, which seems to be any type of meat. I can smell everything now and my vision is sharper. I turn toward the back door after closing the fridge and leave as fast as I can without saying a word to Lucy and disappear into the forest. There is someone I need to chat with. I search for Nicki in the forest for hours then give up when I can't find a trace of her and go to Darla's grave. I sit down at the tree that I carved Darla's initials onto and search through the grocery bag of meat I brought. Before I can dig in, my forearm begins to itch. It drives me crazy so I end up ripping the gauze to shreds. I am shocked to see that the bite mark isn't bleeding at all anymore. Instead I find new sealed skin that looks and feels slightly like scales. It feels like snake's skin to the touch but it doesn't spread, it's a strange scar. I stare at it disgusted that it is my skin. The skin I saw on that monster only a week before, the skin of a Dread.

My stomach grumbles, interrupting my thoughts. I turn to the bag of meat; it's either uncooked or leftover meat. The uncooked one calls to me but I feel safer with the cooked breakfast sausages first. Before I dump the whole container in my mouth I hear someone to my left say, "Cravings are strange aren't they?" I whip my head around to see Nicki standing a few feet away watching me smugly with her arms crossed. I place the sausage container back in the bag with the rest of the meat and stand up. "That smells good, can I have some?" she asks tilting her head toward the bag. I throw it to her, trying to contain my anger. She catches it and looks inside with interest.

"What have you done to me? Why do I suddenly have a craving to attack and eat my sister?" I demand, she looks up from the bag and studies me.

"You're strange you know. Normally when I bite people, they turn. But it takes a week and they are in a coma for the whole change but here you are almost twenty four hours later and you are awake and well walking. The whole eat people thing you'll get used to. After the whole craving blood thing, if you don't you'll eventually go crazy and kill anything that moves."

"You've done something to me. My eyes are weird, my skin and injuries are fully healed, and I'm stronger and have a strange craving for uncooked meat, people and blood. I'm kind of freaking out here." I try to keep my tone even but the anger in my voice is obvious.

"You don't look any different to me Xander. I'm not even sure I turned you- which is strange. I had every intent of doing so- I even bit you." She replies watching me closely suddenly aware that something strange is happening. I take off the sun glasses and her eyes widen. My hazel cat like eyes are equally surprising to her. I bare my retractable fangs angrily at her, a sudden impulse of wanting to snap her neck became very strong but I squash it down. My muscles are tense, if I move I know I would charge at her. She stares at me in surprise. "This can't be." She says slightly horrified taking a step back from me. She waits for me to make a move but I don't.

"What do I do? Is there a cure?" I ask suddenly feeling vulnerable. She shakes her head.

"The venom has bonded with your blood. You can't get rid of it. But I've never seen someone only turn half way. I've only heard of it once but..." she cuts herself off making me wonder about what she was going to say. "Look, after someone is bitten and they turn I come to collect them to the Clan. You have the venom; you're one of us now." She says holding out her hand, beckoning me to come with her. I take a step away from her, shaking my head. "You cannot go back. If the town finds out you've been bitten they will kill you. Everyone will think of you as a monster, especially Conall. Her family hunts Dreads and kills them. Once she finds out she will most likely be the one to kill you. You don't have a choice. You don't belong with them." She tries to convince me.

"No, you turned me into a monster. I will find a way to stay hidden. I'm not going with you. I don't belong with you. I never did." I say taking a step back. Anger fills her eyes and she sneers.

"I was afraid you where going to say that. I know you aren't used to this but you'll see. I'll give you a while to think it over. But you will see that you can't stay there. You will be discovered, secrets in this town never stay hidden, and eventually you will expose yourself- either by killing and feeding off someone or hurting your loved ones. Good luck with that." She says tossing me the container filled with cooked sausage. I blink and next thing I know, she is gone. I wait for about five minutes to see if she would reappear but she doesn't. I open the container and dump it into my mouth and begin to walk home, still feeling hungry.

I put the sun glasses back on and pull the hood over my head, hoping that Nicki is wrong. I take my short cut back where I was bitten only yesterday in the cornfield. I still can't believe what has happened to me. I don't want to believe it. I look up at the sky; the sun's position tells me it's about eight o'clock in the morning. I sigh as I walk toward the High School's football field. I see the team practicing on the field and realize we have Saturday morning practices. I'm excused from them because of my broken rib but it is fully healed now.

I approach the field sprayed black, white, and red lines indicated the field's boundaries in the school colors. 'Wolfsbane High' is spray painted on the ends zone. A sign near by indicates that the school is the 'Home of the Mighty Wolves'. It is the first time I notice this, it must be new. They are gearing up for the Football season. Their first game is a week from today.

Marcus sees me right away, which must not have been hard considering the fact that I'm wearing my school football hoodie. I focus on him, and suddenly notice I can hear what he is saying even though he is on the other side of the field whispering.

"Ureil is over there. The coward claims to have a broken rib. Let's double check, just to make sure." He says, I see the other guys nod. This isn't going to be good. I start to walk from the field only to be blocked by the whole football team; their scent of pumping blood is over powering. I hold my breath and try to ignore their hearts pounding in my ears. "Where do you think you're going Uriel?" Marcus asks tauntingly.

"You know, just taking a walk around town. I'm still new here, just trying to find my way around, guess I took a wrong turn." I say simply turning on my heel to see that I am surrounded by the team. *Oh great. This is gonna get ugly.* I think, trying to make a plan to get away. I remember Nicki's strong grip on me in the forest when she pinned me against the tree. I know I have to get away before I hurt someone like Nicki did when she attacked Anika. Marcus steps forward aggressively.

"Well now coward, you afraid to play because we're too tough for your pretty boy all-star playing?" He challenges. This makes my pride boil angrily within me, I am no coward. A feeling of power courses through my veins, I'm not afraid of them, and I'm not one to back down from a challenge. But I am afraid of what I might do to them if they keep getting in my face.

"I'm not threatened by you. You're just a bully who doesn't know his place." I say through gritted teeth, I feel my fangs threaten to lengthen so I can sink my teeth into him. The thought scares me back into reality.

"Why don't you prove it? Go ahead, put me in my place." He pushes me, which spikes my adrenaline.

"Don't tempt me," I smile, he throws a punch which I dodge quickly. The look on his face is one of confusion. He throws another and another that I continually dodge, the feeling to strike him gets stronger but I push it down, until someone behind me kicks me in the back. It hurts I'm not going to lie, but the hunger in my gut is bursting. All of these guys are bigger than I am but I'm stronger and faster. I flip Marcus on his back and the other guys rush at me. I am hit and kicked but I somehow make it out of the mob, crawling away before I bite someone. I think I'm safe but then I am picked up by the collar of my hoodie. I'm lifted off the ground like and look right into the dark brown eyes of Marcus. He looks pretty ticked off. He punches me square in the face as if I'm a hanging punching bag and I fly to the ground. I spit my blood trying to control myself but give into the anger instead and charge at him faster than he or I can comprehend. I grab his neck and lift him off the ground, I breathe in his scent wanting to rip him apart. It would be so easy. He gasps which brings me back to the present to realize what I am doing. Nicki is right, I have to keep my secret, and right now I am so close to exposing myself. I have to get out of here. I lower him to my eye level, unsure if my eyes are normal or not, but deciding I don't care at the moment.

"Stop coming after me or you will regret it." I growl and I release him. He slumps in a heap on the ground coughing. I turn and pick up my sunglasses that he knocked off my face from the punch. The team watches me in shock as I walk away from the field. I feel good at first but then I realize that no average human could have done that. Marcus was probably double my body weight and I lifted him right off his feet. I need to be more careful. Odds are that with a guy like Marcus, he isn't done with me. I have just embarrassed him in front of his fellow jocks and he now needs to redeem himself. I am getting myself into trouble. How much longer do I have in Wolfsbane before someone figures out my secret and tries to kill me?

Chapter 11: Question

-Anika

I need to clear my head, so I do what I always do when I'm overwhelmed- I go for a walk around town. I walk to the school as if I'm being drawn there. I secretly want to see if Xander is practicing because I remember him telling me he made the team weeks before. I take my time and I'm surprised to see a fight erupt on the field. I stand on the bleachers helplessly looking for Coach Dastin who seems to have disappeared. I cautiously approach the disgruntled team of teenagers looking for Xander but none of them look like him. That's when I see a figure in a 'Mighty Wolves' football letterman jacket crawl out from under the crazed mob. Marcus spots him quickly and lifts the boy to his eye level by the collar of his jacket.

This is when I realize that boy is Xander, I freeze unsure of what to do. These football jocks would never listen to me. They don't even know I exist or they would have realized a girl is gawking at the scene they caused a few yards away.

Suddenly he punches Xander, the force knocking him right out of Marcus's grasp hands. Xander starts bleeding; suddenly, he is on his feet and gets to Marcus unnaturally fast. He grabs the jock by the throat and lifts him from the ground. He speaks to Marcus but I don't hear his words. Then he drops the confused and utterly defeated football captain to the ground and casually picks up his sunglasses and walks away as if nothing had just happened. I stare after him with all the other shocked players.

    Once the shock wears off I run after him, yelling out his name. He has to explain what had just occurred. I notice what direction he's heading I realize where he is going. He is running to my favorite spot. When I get there he has disappeared. I look around only to be disappointed, there's no sight of him anywhere. I sit down at the trunk of my favorite tree and see a figure's shadow. For some reason, I know it's Xander. "You really should think about where to hide before hiding there. You shouldn't be so predictable." I say after a good five minutes of silence. I look up at him after another minute without a reply from him. He watches me intently and exhaustedly through his sunglasses.

"You really shouldn't be here." He says, sounding a tad annoyed and a tad nervous. He looks away from me and focuses on the tree that he is holding onto for balance.

"Oh is that so? Is that because you don't want me here, or because you want to be alone? 'Cause last time I checked, this was my spot first." I reply stubbornly.

"You shouldn't be around me anymore." he says quietly.

"Seriously? Come on Xander. A week ago you wouldn't leave me alone and said you wanted to be my friend. You saved me and now want nothing to do with me?" I say as I start to climb the tree.

"Anika, don't do this. Please don't." he pleads climbing as high as he can go without branches snapping under him.

"What was that on the football field this morning? You were like super human. No one has ever handled Marcus like that."

"I don't know what you're talking about. I wasn't at the field this morning. I'm excused from practice cause of my broken rib."

"If your rib was broken, you wouldn't be climbing trees and hiding from your friends. Let alone picking up an almost fully grown teenager off the ground with your bare hands." I state finally reaching the same branch he is on, he looks uneasy now that I have finally caught up to him. "Xander, you can't lie to me. So just tell the truth."

"I can't." He says stubbornly.

"What do you mean you can't?"

"I just can't."

"Xander, you can tell me anything. What happened five minutes ago?"

"It's nothing. I don't even know what you are trying to get me to say."

"Why are you lying to me?" I ask frustrated, he looks confused at this. "What is it? What's wrong?"

"You can't tell?"

"Tell? Tell what?" He shakes his head at me and takes off his sunglasses.

"Do my eyes seem different to you? Or my teeth, do they seem… pointy?"

"Pointy? They're teeth Xander. They're like knives in your mouth. Everyone has several pointed teeth."

"Yes but do I look different to you?" He asks insistently. I look at him and take in his amazing, normal, golden, hazel eyes- straight, pearly white, normal teeth, tan skin, longish brown hair, high cheek bones, strong jaw line and a few light freckles on the bridge of his nose that you wouldn't notice unless you were up close to him. He looks just like his normal, handsome self aside from the fact he isn't smiling to show off his dimples.

"No, you look normal. Maybe a bit shaken up but Kyle's disappearance has caused everyone to go a little crazy." I say feeling slightly sad about my friend but push the feelings away not wanting to deal with them. Xander's face grows dark and pained.

"What happened to Kyle?" He asks in shock almost losing his balance on the branch.

"He turned right in front of me. He turned into one of them and then broke out of the hospital and was gone in the forest faster than I thought possible. He's gone. He's one of them." My face falls and the feeling of wanting to cry returns. I try to turn away from Xander so he can't see the threatening tears, but next thing I know, I'm free falling from the top of the highest tree in town outside of the forest. I hit a couple branches spinning and knocking me around. Some of the tiny branches cut open my forehead; I hit my head and my leg; I then land on my arm painfully on one tree limb. Everything is a blur, and the only sounds I hear were snapping branches and the thuds of my impact against the tree. Suddenly I'm pushed by a strong force away from the tree and fall straight down to the ground. I close my eyes and embrace for impact but I don't hit the ground. Someone has caught me at the bottom of the tree and is now cradling me in their arms.

My eyes flash open when I realize this, I look up into Xander's face, he looks different. His pupils are abnormally thin like a cat's, his skin seems to pale slightly and he freezes. He stares at me, terror and hunger in his eyes. *What's going on? Why is he staring at me like that? What happened to his eyes? How did Xander catch me all the way down here so quickly?* The questions erupt from my mind; he's staring at the cut on my forehead which is now bleeding slightly. He leans forward then pauses a few inches from my face, then blinks suddenly, as if breaking from a strange trance; his eyes are normal again which bewilders me. I still can't find words. He sets me down on the ground softly and looks at me with horrified eyes. Then he turns and runs.

To my surprise, he sprints straight into the forest and disappears into the midst of the tree trunks with surprising speed. I sit there, staring for a while, unsure of what has just happened. My adrenaline deserts me, oddly I feel little pain- even on my arm which should be broken but only shows a bruise, which makes me feel like I'm going crazier, maybe I hit my head harder than I thought- or something had changed that I am not aware of. The courageous young man I knew a week ago seems to have disappeared and has been replaced by a scared little boy. I feel like I have lost two friends now, two in only forty-eight hours. I close my eyes and suck in a deep breath; I need to talk to my father about what happened in the forest a week ago. Maybe that would calm my mind and give me some answers. I glance back into the forest to see if Xander will appear but there is no such luck. I sigh and stand wiping the twigs and dirt from my jeans and pulling them from my hair while make my way back home.

~ ~ ~

I sit for what feels like hours at the kitchen table waiting for my dad to get home until I don't feel like I can wait any longer. I walk into his study and look for reasons why Xander would suddenly become super fast and stronger than I remember and for symptoms of possible concussions. Kyle's possible cure is on my mind as well. I rummage through all the shelves, skimming books on mythical creatures and plant concoctions that could be a possible cure. I even fire up my dad's old computer but can find nothing. Only explanations of vampires and *'Twilight'* come up in my search which annoys me, what is Twilight any way? Does the rest of the world not know about the Dreaded? We can't be the only town tortured by them. I open Grant Conall's journal to the very last page.

    His story has always bothered me the most. He had disappeared when a new beast had come to the fight with the militia and the Dreads. It looked like a werewolf but acted less like a man and more like an animal with a conscience. To their surprise the beast didn't go after the humans. It only went after the Dreaded. The Dreaded were no match for this beast-for it had killed them with just a scratch of its Copper ingrained claws. (They found a claw that had fallen from the beast when it ran after the Dreads) The Dreads fled and the strange beast ran into the forest after them never to be seen again. The town named the beast the Dread Slayer or the Slayer for short. It had come to the rescue of the town and its people. Grant Conall was never found after that night. Some called him a coward for leaving his militia to die and others thought he had been dragged off into the forest and left for dead. His family, the Conalls, and the Darwin and Ulric families went in the forest after him and hadn't returned until my father and mother and I did with the Darwin family when I was very young. My parents and the Darwins never speak of where we were before we came to Wolfsbane. The Ulric's descendants are gone but the Darwins and the Conalls are still alive.

But my family has had its misfortunes. There is a myth about a curse on my family that the Dunstans had placed for revenge on telling the town their evil secret. They cursed the Conall family that they could only have one child through each generation. And so it has been a straight line. I am the first girl to be born to the Conall line.

Once I get married the Conall family name will disappear.

It makes me sad to think about. My parents have never even acknowledged the myth and have told me that it was nonsense, but I have always wondered why I have never gotten a sibling. My father and his father before him and my grand father had all been the only child. It makes me wonder. Any way, it bothers me that Grant and the Ulric family seems to have just disappeared from the Earth. It never mentions them being found anywhere.

I flip through the pages of the journal until I close the book and look at the back cover that has a huge scratch on the sturdy leather. I wonder if the Slayer scratched it and if the Slayer had killed him. I sigh and place the journal back where I found it in its safe and replace the books I had made a mess of. I then plunk into an arm chair and become so bored that I fall asleep…

~   ~   ~

I see a group of about ten teenagers and twenty adults standing in a circle whispering intensely with serious looks on their faces. I try to get in closer but it doesn't seem to get any clearer. I see the one that looks like he's the leader. He is about as tall as Xander, I guessed he was either eighteen or nineteen, he has wild dirty short platinum blonde hair, enchanting but unafraid gray eyes, chiseled facial features, and his skin is pale. He looks stressed out but he's still very handsome I have to admit. The group looks to him waiting to see his answer.

He clears his throat and then speaks clearly an authoritative voice. "We don't have much time. We must be prepared. The fight for our freedom will be in forty-nine days. I'm sure the Pack Alpha will arrive soon. Until then we prepare and train. We don't stop, we must be ready. It's either our end or theirs. Stay together and back each other up. This is not the time for bickering. This is a time of team work." He looks sternly into each of the group member's eyes. A woman stands out from the crowd with a look of disapproval.

"Asher, we can't afford to wait for the Alpha much longer. He has deserted us along with our strongest Beta. We must appoint another Alpha. You have been standing Alpha for much too long. You should just take your rightful place. You've earned it." The woman also has platinum blonde hair but her eyes are cold.

"Mother we don't have time for this. Alpha will come back. He's never broken a promise. We must not lose faith in our leader. He shall lead us to victory in battle. That is what the Moon has told us." The boy- Asher, replies to his mother, who steps back into her place looking displeased.

"What of the Alpha's daughter?" A girl with long, flowing, scarlet curls asks. She flutters her light brown eyes nervously; they seem to glow in the night. She waits patiently but looks anxious.

"We have no news of her yet. I'm sure she will morph soon. We must be ready to find her. They will try and find her when she is at her weakest point. We have only two weeks before that happens. Be on the look out for suspicious activity among the Dreaded. Knowing the Clan's

Devilin, he is planning something for her." He says with a serious face.

"I'll take first watch with Amber and Cole. We'll see if we can find any more information." A girl with a black pixie cut that is growing into a short bob with lavender highlights states. The scarlet haired girl and a black haired boy step forward as well. Asher nods at them and watches as they leave the group.

"As for the rest of you, let's get moving. We have no time to waste."

~   ~   ~

I wake up with a pounding headache. I rub my temples and wonder why I feel freezing. I head up the stairs to find my mom in the kitchen making dinner. I'm surprised by how long my nap was, five hours. My mother tries to raise her eyebrow at me. "Are you okay? You slept like a log, and you don't look like you're feeling well." She says setting down her spatula and walking over to me. She puts her hand on my forehead and then takes it away. Her hand feels like ice on my skin. "You're burning hot sweet heart." She says looking concerned. I'm not sure what she's talking about, I feel chilled to the bone.

"I'm fine. Have you seen dad?"

"He's working late tonight; he and Chief Darwin went hunting with Jackson." She says returning to her pan and spatula at the stove top. I nod and mumble something about going to back to bed. I lie down and stare at my ceiling, surprised with how much of my strange dream I remember. I can recall the names and faces and what they said. The weird thing was that they all seem familiar. I've heard their names before and have seen similar people before. I wonder if it means anything. I open the calendar and count forty-nine days from now, the date that it land on is October eleventh, a Friday. I wonder what battle they were preparing for. I don't understand what any of it meant. I also notice that twenty two days before the epic battle they spoke of in my dream is my half birthday. I then realize how exhausted I feel and then remember the possibility that it could have been only just a simple, random dream. I go back to my bed and close my eyes allowing sleep to overtake me.

The weekend goes by quickly with no sign of my dad returning home from his search in the woods. It's the twenty-sixth of August, a Monday now. It is the first day of me returning to school and my normal-but-extremely-abnormal existence. I leave my house early this morning wanting to see if I can catch Xander before school but as it turns out, he is gone. The whole day of school he never shows up. I wonder if he went home sick. As English rolls around I begin to get distracted. *Where was he? What is he doing? Why isn't he at school? Does it have something to do with the Football team?* My friend Melanie nudges my shoulder bringing me back to class. I look at her as if I was asking her why she did so. She has honey colored, extremely long hair that she always straightens. She has fair skin and bright blue eyes. She's usually kind to everyone and has a good sense of humor. Everyone loves to be around her and she has a talent for anything musical, especially the piano and singing.

She points at the teacher, Mrs. Angelo, who is watching me with an un-amused look on her face. Mrs. Angelo is my favorite teacher and I, her favorite student, but she always hates it when people doze off during her lectures. She is a shorter, Latino woman. She's normally kind and funny but if she feels disrespected she gets feisty. Let's just say that she isn't pleasant to be around when she gets angry. She clears her throat. "Anika, the answer please?" She asks trying not to glare.

"Sorry, what was the question?" I ask feeling my face redden.

"What was the type of style that Ralph Waldo Emerson's wrote his most famous works?" She repeats.

"Transdentalism," I reply and she nods at me.

"Very good, now pay attention." She mumbles continuing on with her lecture. I turn to Melanie and give her a look of thanks.

"What's up with you today? You seem to be absent minded." She says looking concerned.

"I've just had a lot on my mind." she nodded with understanding. She has been scared out of her mind for me after the accident had occurred. I feel bad for worrying her; she is a good friend to have. We have mostly the same classes so she got me all the homework and gave it to me when I was in the hospital recuperating.

After school gets out I head home and finish my homework and do all my chores then I go to sit down and read for a while when I hear a knock at the door. I open it and am surprised to see Mason standing in the door way.

"Hey Mason, what's up?" I ask smiling in surprise; he shifts uncomfortably from foot to foot like his brother has so many times before. He looks up at me with his electric blue worried eyes.

"I was wondering if you had seen Xander anywhere." He says seriously, my smile disappeared.

"No, I haven't seen him sense Saturday morning when I went for a walk." I say feeling my stomach flip with nervousness.

"Oh, we last saw him on Saturday too but he hasn't come home sense. Would you mind keeping an eye out for him and telling him that he needs to come home if you happen to find him?"

"Of course."

"Thank you, Anika. It would mean a lot. Have a good afternoon." He says shoving his hands in his pockets and walking away. I close the door and feel a sickening feeling in my stomach. *Now Xander's missing too?* I can't believe it, I feel worried and exhausted and again a horrid headache settles in my temples. I sit down with a bowl of Rocky-Road Ice cream and rub them. Things seem to be getting worse, not better. I hope that things would all return to normal soon.

Chapter 12: Missing
-Xander

I wake up in a dark room with fancy red, stiff carpet and an old rotting dresser, a couple of broken cushioned chairs, and a closet. My head aches and I feel the blood rushing to my head. I sit up feeling sick and but for once not hungry. White and black dots dance across my vision. I shake my head to get rid of them and push my hand through my hair, and then I slowly, carefully stand up using the wall to steady me. I look around the room wondering where in the world I am. I see a door in the opposite corner of the room and open it. There is a large, dark, empty hall way. *Where am I? How did I get here?*

I wander around this giant maze of a structure that turned out to be a huge mansion. It even has its own opera house. I look outside to see it's in the middle of the forest surrounded by dying trees, dry dirt, and thorns patches. I turn a corner and enter onto the stage of the opera house. It's dark, the only light is coming from candles. I see figures sitting in the chairs in the audience. Only one in the front was empty, and it has my name scratched into its wooden back rest. Tons of beady black and yellow cat eyes reflect off the dim candle light toward me. Even though it is pitch black I can see all of them in detail.

My attention is torn from the crowd when I hear footsteps to my left. Coming from stage right is Nicki in full Dread form, scales and all. She smiles wickedly at me until she gets to center stage. Suddenly a stinging, burning pain erupts in my skull and I hear her voice in my head and watch her mouth not move once. *Come, stand next to me and say hello to your Clan.* She holds out her hand and I clutch my head falling to my knees in pain. I hiss at her, baring my fangs in defiance. *I said come Xander.* She whispers in my head again, facing me now and turning her head. Suddenly I find myself moving against my will, crawling toward her on the stage. I fight with all my might only to have a raging head ache and a burning flame in my blood. I release out a growl that echoes through the opera house. No one in the audience moved. The burning and headache doesn't stop until I collapse at center stage next to

Nicki. "Was that so hard?" She whispers aloud ruthlessly.

I glare at her and slowly pull myself to a standing position. "Now Xander, we have given you time to see how you would do without us. The Conalls already suspect something is wrong with you. They will hunt you down and kill you if you don't stay with us. So make your decision. Stay with us… or die." She says her voice echoes, the hall is completely silent even though it's filled with Dreads that currently look human despite their eyes, they all sit motionless, their eyes glassy as if there is no one occupying their minds. I step away from her.

"If I don't stay with you, you are going to kill me?" I ask my voice full of disbelief. She looks at me rather seriously, but does not answer my question.

"What is your choice?" She demands. I glower at her, tensing myself up knowing what is coming.

"I will never be like you." I growl, my words echo hauntingly through the theatre, she growls making a strange guttural sound. My head hurts again, and I hear her voice in my head clearly, *"Very well, you must have a death wish. Allow me to grant it."* She lets out an ear popping roar, and the audience returns it, all turning into full Dreaded form and looking at me. She lunges at me and the rest all leap from their seats following her lead. I run from the stage ignoring the pain pulsing in my head and her voice telling me that I should just give up and let them tear me into pieces.

I sprint faster through the halls feeling the pounding of the hundreds of feet on the floor chasing after me. I see a window at the end of the hallway and pick up speed, surprised at how much faster I am than they are. I jump through the window, shattering the glass, and land on my feet now sprinting through the forest. I ignore the stinging pain of the glass shards sticking into my skin as I fly through the trees and dodge logs on foot feeling like an action hero. My head and blood still burns as I fight against Nicki's will. *"You are a fool. We offer you fellowship, and you turn it away.*

You will die for your stupidity. I will give you one last chance Xander. Two weeks. If you manage to stay hidden that long you will see you cannot stay there. We will come to town and collect you. If you refuse us we will kill you, but if we come to town, people will die. It's your choice. You are running into Slayer territory. If you run in there they will kill you for us. Just stop where you are. Trust me." I shake her voice from my head only hearing lies and continue running in the same direction. Soon the thundering footsteps cease and I am alone. I keep running trying to find my way out of this labyrinth of a forest.

    I finally realize that it would be smart to climb a tree to see where town is. It's now the dead of night. I can see the outline of the trees and the roots springing up from the ground. I find a tree that has branches that are perfect for climbing; I shoot up the tree with ease until I get to the top. The forest stretches for miles and miles. *How did I get here?* I wonder, I look around until I see lights in the far distance. I'm a long way from Wolfsbane, in the heart of the woods. I can see a huge cliff and I hear the faint sound of a waterfall.

It might lead me closer to town. I climb down the tree and walk toward the direction of the sound; soon the smell of fresh water hits my nostrils. I'm so close; I come upon a shallow river and walk across it to the other side. The water is freezing and stings my ankles.

    Once I get to the other side I think it will be wise to stick with where the river flows, this small river runs down from the mountains. I come to a crossroads. One river goes to my right, the other keeps flowing straight. I was going to follow it to my right when I suddenly feel like I'm in danger. I hear a growl to my right and turn slowly toward the sound. There stands a huge wolf like creature on its hind legs sniffing the air. The moon now shows down on its claws making them gleam a strange color, copper. The animal reminds me of what I saw in the book Anika showed to me. *A Slayer.* I recall, it was tall, about six or seven feet tall, with a long tail, a broad black furred chest, white fur covering the rest of its body and its eyes are bright silver. It watches me, growling until it lets out a long, ear bursting howl.

I take off running only to hear several other howls respond. It gallops after me quickly, followed by more of them. *You've got to be kidding me, there's a pack of them!* I panic running next to the river that flows relatively straight. I pick up speed when I hear the sound of a waterfall and rushing water. The growling disappears in the sound of falling water. I notice that there are no more trees in front of me and the river just seems to end next to me. I begin to drop and I realize I had run right off a huge cliff.

I freak out and grab a rock on the edge of the cliff, smacking into the rock wall so I won't fall into the black abyss below me, water rumbles as it is swallowed by the darkness far beneath me. I feel small rocks and dirt fall on my head which makes me look up to see three Slayers scratching at me and barely missing by inches. The white one in the middle is the biggest, the other two are smaller, one blonde, the other red. Their silver eyes look at me with hatred and hunger. I have to think fast. I look across the cliff to the other side. If I don't jump they will claw and rip me to pieces.

I start to swing, I feel the rocks cutting into my skin and it burns. I ignore the pain and push off with my legs, propelling myself into the air. I reach out and barely catch a tree root that has grown out of the side of the rocky cliff. The white Slayer howls, baring its fangs at me. They weren't done with me. They run another way knowing that there must be an easier way to cross the ravine. I waste no time and hurry to climb up the tree roots. Once I pull myself up onto the ground I sprint through the forest sensing that town is near. I don't stop until I find my house and open the back door with the spare key we keep under the mat. Once I close the door I collapse to the floor with exhaustion.

~ ~ ~

I wake to a sudden cold freezing liquid being poured on my face. I open my eyes to see my family staring down at me wide-eyed. I cough and realize Mason has dumped a cup of water on my head. I sit up, shaking my head and whipping the water off when I realize my hand is bleeding and has rocks and slivers of wood sticking out of the skin. My family doesn't move, only stares. I must be really dirty, my jeans are caked with mud and fallen leaves and I have scratches on my arms and neck. My shirt has dirt, blood, and sweat all over it. I stand up and go to the sink and wash my hands. I see why they are staring. My hair is messy and dirty, so is my face and I have blood around my mouth. I rinse my face and when I wash the blood off my hands I see that new skin has already grown and it's as if I was never cut. I dry my face and turn to my family who are still looking at me like I'm some kind of alien from another planet. I stand there unsure of what to do or say. My mom is the first to move, she hugs me so tight I can't breathe. I hug her back, wondering how long I've been gone. "Where have you been Xander? You've had me worried sick!" She cries.

"It's okay mom, I'm here." I whisper. My father also pulls me in his arms and soon my whole family is hugging me.

"Don't you dare do that again!" My dad says gruffly.

"What did I do exactly?" I ask when my mother releases me to go and get ready for her job as Mayor Rune's assistant. My father is acting Sheriff of the town now that both the Sheriff and the Deputy are out looking for the missing people and apparently I have been added to their list of people to look for. He tells me I have been missing for a week and there have been three more disappearances, Kaleb from the football team is one of them. *How have I been missing for almost a whole week and why I can only recall last night? What did I do? Where did I go?*

I remember walking into the forest after catching Anika when she fell out of the tree but the rest after that is fuzzy, I then wondered what or whose blood had covered my face and shirt, because it had not been my own. I guess that's what Nicki meant when she said if I didn't feed I'd lose control and kill someone. I suddenly find myself terrified again, I have to figure out what I killed, no wonder I'm hungry anymore. My father insists that I tell him what happened but I can't remember.

My father isn't the only one who is frustrated with my memory. Mason is also angry with me. It's as if he thinks I had planned on going back to California and left him here in this crazy town. He gives me the silent treatment, but I can tell he is secretly relieved that I'm back safely. I play with Lucy for a little while until she and Mason have to go to school- she is homeschooled with a friend due to the fact that the town has deemed our house unsafe and that my parents both work and can't home school her themselves.

She seems to be the only one not upset with me- which is nice, but after she leaves the house is empty. Everyone else has either gone to work or school, it's a Friday so I don't really want to go to school and face all of the questions of people that wonder what happened and where I went for a week. I don't even know the answers to those questions. I decide to go to school anyway. I have lots I need to make up.

I shower and wash all the dirt and dry blood out of my hair and off my skin and hurry to get dressed in clean clothes. If I run to school I'd still have thirty minutes left in my Chemistry class and be on time for all of the other ones. I sprint to school and run straight to class. I take a deep breath before opening the door. When I enter the room, surprised, curious eyes watch me. Even Coach Dastin stops in mid sentence at the sight of me. Anika's reaction surprises me the most. She looks confused but relieved as she pulls out my chair for me. After the relief has dissipated she watches me suspiciously.

Her eyes ask me *where have you been and how are you back?* I smirk at this and keep my eyes on my chair feeling a sense of panic all of the sudden. Nicki's voice echoes in my head: *If Anika finds out she will be the one who kills you.* I force the thought from my mind and sit in my chair, not daring to look in Anika's direction. She watches me looking hurt and confused. I find myself wishing I had stayed in the forest; it would have made my life a lot less complicated. The bell rings and I get up from my seat and try to walk quickly from the room, almost running to my next class.

Chapter 13: Realization
-Anika

He ran from the room. The whole class watches in awe. I still can't believe he is back. I'm both relieved and shocked. He is the first one in history to ever come out of that forest after missing for a week on his own, alive, and in one piece. After I snap out of the shock the bell rings again bringing me and the rest of my chemistry class back to Earth. I run to my English class knowing I'm late. I can't focus in English again. I keep getting distracted with my own thoughts on Xander. *What happened? How is he back? Did my father find him? Why was he acting so strange? He seemed afraid of me, but why?* My brain is buzzing with these questions. I need to talk to someone but Melanie won't understand the Dread part of my life, Lani is practically nonexistent since Kyle's transformation. She's only a shell of her former self and is in and out of school. My father has been gone for a week now on the search, and my mother seems to be extra busy helping around town. There is no one I can talk to and I am going crazy.

Another two weeks go by like this. I only see my father twice those weeks and my mother would get home around one in the morning so I never got the chance to see her. Now it's Friday the thirteenth. I wouldn't call it a 'lucky day,' but it's a town holiday, the day that the early town's people were saved by the Slayer. We call it Wolves day, we used to call it Slayer Day but Mayor Rune said that it was politically incorrect and changed it, taking yet another thing from our town's traditions. I grumble as I get out of bed. I am in no mood for festivities.

I drag myself to the garage to get my bike; my family is one of the few that own cars. We have two; a black Dodge Ram truck, and my father's police car. I'm one of the few kids that were taught how to drive. Our town is so small that we all walk or ride bikes to the places we need to go because it's so close. Sometimes I get a glimpse of the outside world and what it's like. No one has fancy flat screen televisions except the

Uriel's and only the important people and the school gets computers. I feel like we are about ten years behind everyone else. Especially when I saw Xander's phone the first day he was here. A touch screen, he called it an iphone. I wonder if the outside world has flying cars yet and why we never updated with the rest of the world except through television or rarely the internet which no one really uses because they viewed it as a big waste of time. Mayor Rune says we don't need contact with the outside world, his father said the same, as did his grand father. For some reason the Mayoral position has always lands to one of the members of his family line. They cut off our connection with the world and he and his assistant were the only ones that had contact with towns beyond our own, making us rely on him.

    I get on my bike and ride it to school. On my way there I think of Xander and his family, what a big change this must have been for them. We use paper more than we did computers and we have phones that seem to be thirty years behind their family's electronics. I feel bad for them, trying to fit in but sticking out like a sore thumb here. Then their son disappears and then reappears suddenly and acts all strange. I don't understand why he would act this way.

Maybe something happened in the forest that he hasn't told anyone. He looks pretty shaken up and his now long, dark, wavy hair covered his eyes and his stubble has grown a little. He acts like he just wants to be ignored with his hood up and walking quickly everywhere he goes, but he gets the opposite of ignored being the most attractive guy in a small school, let alone a small town, where everyone watches his every move. He must feel like an ant under a microscope.

I lock up my bike and head to chemistry. There he is sitting at his desk immersed into what looks like today's assignment. I notice he finishes it quickly being smarter than I ever thought he was. This makes me confused because he asked me multiple times for help before and this was one of the hardest units we are learning. I can barely understand it. *Has he been playing dumb the whole time? Why?*

Then I realize that the first words he had ever spoken to me were asking if he could cheat off my assignment. I sit down as I connect the dots. *So that's how he first got to see how I was without getting nervous about introducing himself. Even the most confident guy is afraid of girls.* I realize looking over at him when he sets his pencil down and picks up his now finished assignment. He looks over at me in surprise to see how intently I've been watching him. He gives me a fake smirk that doesn't reach his eyes and stands up and hands Coach Dastin his assignment before abruptly leaving the room in a hurry.

Dastin looks over at me with a look of confusion on his face, a look that I return and shrug in reply to. *Why is he avoiding me?* I wonder in frustration, letting out a huge sigh that releases some of my inner tension. "Today class is Wolves Day. As you all know, we will have a brief lesson and then you are excused for the rest of the day to enjoy the holiday's festivities such as the parade and the football game later tonight. Conall, go get the copies of the notes and assignments for today for me." he demands.

I nod, get up from my seat and hurry into the hallway. I look for Xander, but he is no where to be found. I go to the office to grab copies for Coach Dastin and head back into the hall. I didn't realize that Dastin needs so many copies of our assignment. The stack is so high it touches my chin when I carry it in my arms. I'm all wobbly and sometimes worried about them falling all over the floor. I turn a corner and I trip over someone else's foot sending papers flying everywhere. I feel the person catch me lightly but quickly by the waist and help set me back on my feet. "I'm so sorry! Are you okay?" says a voice that I've missed for weeks now. I turn to see Xander's golden eyes looking into mine, half shocked, half concerned. I freeze, suddenly hyper-aware of everything going on around me, especially the fact that Xander's arm is still wrapped around my waist holding me up. "Anika, breathe." He says making me realize that I've been holding my breath. I inhale and he releases my waist. I look around the hall to see paper strung everywhere.

"Oh no, this is going to take forever." I sigh kneeling starting to pick up the papers and stack them. Xander bends down to help me with them, avoiding my eyes. I don't look at him until I find a couple pages that I think are strange. They have symbols I have never seen before; they swirl toward the middle of the page. Most of the pages are like this. Out of the whole stack only one hundred pages are the actual assignment. I look up at Xander who is now watching me. I show him the paper and he looks at it in surprise. I turn it back to me and study it more closely. I try to decipher the symbols but it doesn't make sense. The longer I look at it, the symbols start moving. Swirling until I start from the edge of the paper followed the symbols to the middle. A picture starts forming; *it has a girl that suddenly turns into a Slayer. Then there are monsters, Dreads and strange bat creatures. A boy is shown bitten and transforming but leaving the Dreads. The two are then together and running through the forest and the boy is surrounded by other Slayers on one-side with strange winged people and Dreads with strange bat creatures on the other with the Slayer girl reaching out to him.* Suddenly I am being shaken and the picture stops moving and once again becomes the swirl of strange symbols on the page. I look up at Xander who is looking at me with worry in his eyes.

"Anika, are you okay?" He asks. I nod as I fold up the piece of paper and stick it in my back pocket. We begin to pick up the papers quickly.

"Why aren't you in class?" I ask not facing him.

"I just need some time to think." He says, sorting the assignments from the random symbol filled papers.

"Think about what?" I ask watching him now as I hold the assignments in my hand while he picks up the rest of the stack and carries it for me.

"This town, life, and how I never should have doubted you. I should have believed you about the Dreads. I'm sorry." He says looking at his shoes.

"It's okay, we all learn from our mistakes." I try to smile but it falls from my face and is covered by confusion. He walks back to chemistry and I follow him. I open the door but he pushes it back with his back to allow me inside first like a gentleman and offers me a small shy smile. I smile back in appreciation. Dastin looks at the two of us and raises an eye brow.

"I was wondering what took Conall so long with the copies. Looks like she even brought you back to class Uriel." he says looking content as if that was why he really sent me out into the hallway. Xander shrugs and places them on Dastin's desk. When the Coach moves to pick up the papers his face turns slightly red as if it's really hard to pick up and hold. I don't remember them being that heavy. Even Xander lifted them easily. Dastin sets the copies in his closet and locks the door which I find strange. "Our lecture is over, grab your homework and go to today's festivities with your families." he says seriously and everyone runs to the front of the room, grabs a homework sheet and stampede into the hallway. Xander has disappeared in the midst of the chaos and it's just Coach Dastin and me.

"What were those papers for?" I ask tilting my head at his locked closet. He hesitates.

"I've always fascinated by this town's history. I found these strange writings in a book in the library that was hidden in a chest in the attic of the school so I sent them to my cousin to decipher but she needed the book so she faxed me the pages. My cousin says they are an ancient prophecy sent from the moon to the Slayers when they first saved the town. I was planning on showing it to your father; you know how much he likes monsters." He says stiffly.

"Well the festivities are about to start, we'd better get going." He says herding me toward the door and locking it behind him.

~ ~ ~

I want nothing to do with the town's "Wolves-day" Festival. Instead I go straight home and try to forget what the town has planned on the Mayor's new celebration. The one nice thing about the whole day is the surprise of finding my dad in the Armory when I got home. He looks determined but his eyes soften when they see me. "Hey Dad," I smile as I walk in; he gives me a grin and a quick hug before returning to a bag and filling it with weapons. "Why are you taking all of that ammo?" I ask raising an eyebrow. He continues loading it up as he answers me.

"We went into the woods; Dreads are everywhere, just laying in wait, watching the town. As if they are waiting to strike, but when? We've been hunting for days; there are always more of them, no sign of any of the missing people." He says zipping the bag and slinging it over his shoulder.

"There is someone who came back about two weeks ago." I say picking up my bow and arrows. My father's muscles tense and he pauses when he hears this.

"Someone made it back alive?"

"Yes, and all in one piece. He is completely unharmed except for a couple scratches and bruises."

"Who?" My father demands facing me now.

"Xander Uriel. The boy that rescued me when Kyle was…." I stop myself, not daring to say more. The pain from Kyle's transformation is still there and it pierces my heart to think about it. My father shakes his head in disbelief.

"That boy should be dead. How in the world did he survive out there for a week? How did I not see him?" He rubs his eyes irritably, and then sighs. "We are going back in the woods tonight. I'm sorry to be gone so much. I hope we can get to the bottom of this. This whole search and rescue thing is a lost cause. The missing people are gone. If they were still alive they would have arrived with the Uriel boy." He says picking up the bag and heading for the door.

"Father, wait," he pauses. "Something is happening to me. I keep getting these strange dreams and headaches and I always feel really cold but mom says I'm burning hot, I'm constantly hungry, and my limbs hurt and my jaw has been aching and I'm having the worst growing pains. I asked mom about it but she doesn't know what's going on. I thought maybe you would know, I'm kinda freaking out so if you knew anything I would be grateful if you could tell me something."

He watches me for a while and does not say anything until he smiles. "Our family is unique Anika. We are natural born hunters. We have instincts built in us and at some point we grow into them. It can never be guessed when we grow into them because everyone is ready at different times. I didn't grow into mine until I was about fourteen, it runs in our blood. How can we hunt well if we don't have a tiny bit of animal in us?" He winks and I swear I see his eyes flash silver before turning blue like they normally are. "Don't worry about it; it's natural for us Conalls." He says turning and leaving. I stand there staring at the door. What my father said makes no sense. It's like a strange riddle or something. I look at my bow in my hands and grip it harder. I need to think, and the shooting range is the perfect place for it.

I get into my dad's truck which he leaves the keys in for me, obviously knowing that I was going to head to the range. I start the engine and drive slowly into town, avoiding the parades and the school grounds where the parties are taking place.

~ ~ ~

I nock one of my copper arrows and lift the bow. I aim as I pull back the string, trying to focus on one question in my mind at a time. I release the arrow; it soars through the air until it hits its target with a thump noise. I do this over and over, trying to sort through my thoughts. *My father's riddles were so strange. I didn't understand what he was trying to tell me. He picked his words carefully, watching what he told me and keeping it extremely vague. Why would he keep things from me? Was it my next step in training to become a hunter? What did he mean by 'it's normal' and 'the Conall blood is unique'? He said we were born with instincts that don't fully develop until the time is right. And his eyes, I know my fathers eyes and they are sky blue. But for a second I saw them flash silver. How is that possible? Was I hallucinating? I seem to be doing that a lot lately…*

I let my thoughts flow along with all of the arrows I'm shooting. Each arrow I release makes me feel calmer but doesn't give me any answers. I decide to switch my focus to Xander. *Why is he acting so weird? What happened in the woods? Why has he changed so dramatically? Why was he asking weird questions like if his teeth were pointy? Why did he act so afraid of me when he got back? How did he beat up Marcus as if he were a rag doll on the field? Why? Why? Why?*

The questions keep coming like an avalanche but I have no answers. My thoughts begin to quicken, my shooting does as well. I end up shooting one quickly after another then another then another. Eventually I shoot more than one that all land super close to the target. I become frustrated and start shooting more arrows, this time they all but hit what I'm aiming for. I grunt and demand for my brain to think of answers.

Come on think! I scream in my head, I sling my bow over my shoulder and start to pick up all of my arrows to put them in the quiver when a memory floods my brain. I remember Xander and me in the tree before he disappeared. I fell and he caught me impossibly fast and he beat up Marcus with inhuman strength. His skin had paled and he looked at me in only one way something has ever looked at me after he caught me. I realize his pupils looked like a cat's would, just like a Dread's eyes. All the sudden everything makes sense.

A feeling of danger settles on me. I feel as if I'm being watched and followed. My mind is exploding as it put this puzzle together. *Xander was also bitten by a Dread. He was turning but it was before he disappeared. That must be why he survived in the woods for a week but the Dreads never let their prey out of their sight or one of their own to wander around. The Clan always stayed together. So why was he not with them?* But none of these questions matter. He is turning, just like Kyle. Now two people I care about have now been taken from me by monsters.

Chapter 14: Choose
-Xander

The past few weeks since I've returned have been busy. After school I disappear into the corn fields and into the forest where I try to figure out this newly found part of myself. I learn that I can see things in perfect detail, any thing that moves catches my attention, including ants on the forest floor ten yards away from me. I'm also at least ten times stronger and faster than I was; I test it out on a newly fallen log. I lift it with little difficulty and hold it above my head, doing a couple reps with it before setting it down and feeling more energized instead of exhausted. All of my senses seem to increase when I am in Dread mode. I feel stronger and more aware but I'm also afraid. I don't know my own strength or my hunger and I fear that I will hurt someone. Nicki's voice in my head frightens me the most. She has some control over me if I am too angry, frightened, or aggressive. I know she has been keeping tabs on me, sometimes I can feel when she is nearby. The closer she is, the clearer her voice in my head is and the more painful the stinging my headaches get. I try to stay as far away from her as possible. She can control it but can I? Can I contain this monster inside me? Several times, especially when I'm angry, hungry, or tired I will randomly transform without wanting to or thinking about it. I need to have better control my emotions if I want to control myself. I've trained myself over the weeks, hunting and feeding on animals to keep my hunger under control, testing my senses, my strength, my power and fighting ability and at times I get brave enough to try and get close to Nicki to see if I can maintain control. If I am going to survive in Wolfsbane I will have to watch myself and not let her get in my head.

    I walk in the forest concentrating on my sense of hearing while hunting when I began to notice a faint thumping noise. I follow it until I come upon the smell of fear and anger, which tastes like sodium and bitter soap mixed with the scent of a human. As I emerge from the trees I see an area that is clear of weeds and has several targets. It has dirt floor and has a line painted in white and a girl standing right behind it aiming at a target that held lots of arrows already on and surrounding it. The girl lowers her bow and walks to the target then pulls the arrows out roughly. I know who the girl is when I had stumbled upon the scent.

Anika looks around until she spots me standing at the edge of the forest. She quickly lifts her bow from her shoulder and tries to put an arrow on it but drops it instead. I have obviously startled her. Eventually she finally gets the arrow on the string of her bow and pulls back aiming it at me.

"Stop where you are and don't come any closer." She says sternly, a bead of sweat falls from her brow. She knows that it's me but she still aims at me. I stop but look at her in confusion. *Why is she aiming at me?* I wonder, a distinct scent of bitter soap hits my taste buds, she is afraid of me. *She knows.* I hold up my hands and take a small step back.

"Anika, calm down and just breathe." I say slowly, eyeing the arrow that is aimed right at my chest. The tip gleams of copper.

"Shut up," she commands seriously not taking her eyes off her target.

"You wouldn't shoot your friend would you?" I ask taking a step toward her, she doesn't move, I can hear her heart beat increase.

"I said don't move!" she shouts angrily, I take another, shaky step towards her and she releases the arrow, barely tilting the bow slightly to the left making the arrow sail over my shoulder instead of sinking it into my chest. I feel the air on my neck as it whistles past, it's a warning shot. "You were bitten weren't you?" she accuses. I say nothing. "Answer me Xander." she demands, loading another arrow onto the bow string. I have no choice; I slowly lower my hands and push up the sleeve on the arm that was bitten, showing her the scale-like skin that has scarred on my forearm. I look up at her with sad eyes; there is no taking it back now. Her eyes widen. She stares into my eyes, the sadness plain to see in her own. Tears leak from her eyes and fall on her cheeks, she does not move from her position of aiming at me.

"Are you going to kill me?" I ask, looking her right in her eyes. Conflict is plain to see in them. This will not be easy for her. I'm not going to run, that would be cowardly and I know she will chase me down anyway. I don't move. I only watch her, waiting for her to make her move.

"I can't," she whispers lowering her bow looking ashamed and staring at my shoes. *What does she mean she can't?* I wonder.

"I won't hurt you…" I don't say anything else because I know it doesn't matter. "I haven't hurt anyone." I slowly take a step forward. She doesn't move her lowered bow. She only looks into my eyes; hers now dried from the tears. She looks more numb than upset now. She watches me carefully but doesn't make any move to aim at me. I take a few more steps until I'm in front of her.

"When did this happen?" She whispers quietly,

"The day you finally woke up in the hospital, after I saw you I went to go bury Darla… Nicki appeared and attacked me. She was in human form but started turning into a monster and that's when she bit me. I ran home and cleaned the wound but passed out and when I woke up I was this… thing." I explain, covering my strange scar protectively.

"Why didn't you end up in the hospital like Kyle? When Kyle transformed he was pure… monster." She recalls gazing into the woods lost in memory.

"I don't know… I only get the eyes, fangs, senses and strength of one." I reply. Her eyes harden when she looks at me.

"Nicki did this?" she asks, I nod slowly.

"She truly is a monster, that means I'm not crazy and I'm not seeing things." she spits angrily. That's when painful stinging in my head comes, I yell out in pain grabbing my head and falling to my knees. Nicki is close, and her whisper is loud in my head. *I knew you wouldn't last long.* Her cruel voice echoes. Anika kneels down beside me and takes my face in her hands. She mouths something like 'What's happening?' but I can't hear her because my ears were ringing. She takes a step back, her eyes widen and I realize that I must be in Dread state. Out of the corner of my eye I see movement and shift my body in front of Anika to guard her.

"Load your bow. We've got company." I say gruffly but it sounds muffled in my ears. I turn to see Nicki approaching the shooting range in human form. Her eyes flick from me to Anika. I catch the scent of rotten eggs coming off her and sense jealously. I stand up protectively in front of Anika, putting a wall between Nicki and her. I stiffen as I see her reinforcements emerge behind her from the forest. *This is not good.* I think backing closer to Anika.

I recognize a few of the Dreads. Victor and Kaleb are among them. They are huge and so overly muscular it looks painful and unnatural. Their empty Dread eyes watch us hungrily, waiting for Nicki's command to attack. There are so many of them. Nicki is building up an army. I look all of them in the eyes, daring them to come at me first. Surprisingly Anika is the first to speak.

"You will pay for your actions." She growls aiming an arrow right between Nicki's eyes. Nicki looks at her with an evil grin, as if it's her plan to make Anika suffer.

"Xander, you're one of us. Come and join us and bring the girl. We will dispose of her together! If she lives she will hunt you down until she knows you're dead. Join your Clan and forget your other life. You cannot have it now. If you refuse to bring her and join us we will slaughter you both. Again, it's your choice." She looks at Anika hungrily. Her eyes flicker to me now. *She thinks you're a monster.* Nicki's voice taunt in my head. I'm too angry to feel the sting in my head this time. What Nicki said had hurt deep, I look back at Anika who is watching Nicki, anger and fear conflict in her eyes. The tension between the Dreads and us is heavy. Anika looks at me as if waiting for my reply. I look at Nicki once more knowing my answer. *This is your last chance. I will not give you anymore after this and I will find a way to kill you if you don't join me.* Nicki's voice is full of venom in my head.

"No." I say simply.

"Excuse me?" Nicki asks appalled, both Nicki and Anika look shocked by my answer.

"I cannot accept your offer." I repeat, Anika looks relived but that's when all heck breaks loose. Nicki makes that strange guttural growl she made when I last saw her and the Dreads charge. The ground shakes from the stampede of Dreads thundering toward us. Anika starts shooting arrows and only some of them fall, but there are too many. I throw Anika over my shoulder and start sprinting. "Shoot them down! I'm getting us out of here!" I command. She obeys without question or hesitation. We race through the woods with alarming speed; she shoots down any Dread that gets too close to us.

Everything is going well until Anika's arrows run out. Nicki slams into me sending both Anika and me flying through the air. We hit the ground and my head spun, I gasp for air and jump up and cradling Anika in my arms. I take off again and she is gasping for air, she had fallen pretty hard. "My bow," She coughs.

"No time to get it, I need to get you to safety." I say picking up speed. I'm getting nervous; she's still having difficulty breathing- she passes out in my arms. I look up to see the edge of the forest just ahead of us. I need to get across that line. *I will get you. You had your chance. I will keep my promise. You will die by my hand and so will Anika. She will die before you so you will know what heartbreak feels like, to want someone you can never have. Watch your back.* I hear Nicki say but I block her voice from my mind as I cross the line into the town. I run to my house.

My parents look alarmed when they see Anika passed out in my arms. *I have some major explaining to do.* I think. "Xander what happened?" my father demands as I set Anika on the sectional in the basement.

"Monsters in the forest attacked us. I out ran them but they won't give up on trying to get me in their grasp so they can kill me. I had to get her to safety." I say looking at them in the eyes.

"What? That's crazy! Are you feeling okay? You've been acting weird since you got home after missing for a week. You never talk to us anymore." my mother states getting emotional.

"I know what I saw mom." I take a blanket and put it on Anika who is still out cold. "Even Mason saw one of them."

"I don't know what I saw and neither do you." he says angrily.

"Xander's right. There are monsters in the forest. I see them when I look out the window sometimes. They always watch our house." Lucy says and we all freeze. *Oh no. They really are watching me. I'm putting everyone in danger by living here.* A pit forms in my stomach, I feel sick.

"They watch the house because they want to kill me." I say putting my face in my hands. My family looks at me like I'm a lunatic. "I can prove it. But you have to promise not to tell anyone, and not to treat me different. You guys said you will always love me. This is where you prove it." I take a deep breath, they all promise and I transform. My mother screams, Lucy stares in shock with Mason and my father reaches for his gun. "They want to kill me because I didn't join them. And now I've put you all in danger. I'm so sorry. If you want me to leave I understand but know that I love you all very much. I know this is shocking and scary, I'm scared too but I wouldn't do anything to hurt you." I say looking them in the eyes. At first, no one moves. I think my dad is going to shoot me. Lucy runs to me and hugs me.

"Just because you are kind of a monster now doesn't mean you're not still my brother." She says crying and not letting go. I hug her back, surprised at her reaction. The whole family follows Lucy, soon we are in a big group hug despite the fact that I look like a monster.

"You will always be our son." My mother whispers.

Chapter 15: Responsibility
-Anika

"Nothing will be the same. Not for you, or me, or the pack." The darker haired boy said to Asher. They are alone; Asher is pacing back and forth.

"I know Cole. You don't have to tell me that. Time is running out. The pack is getting restless. Tensions between us and the Dreaded are getting higher. We all know what's coming. I'm contemplating going into that wretched town, and bringing the Alpha and the best Beta and their families here myself." Asher says gruffly, stopping his pacing and facing the boy named Cole.

Cole is as calm as stone. "We cannot wait forever, but I know both you and I feel that it isn't the right time to strike. I'm your most trusted friend, I have never been wrong about things like this. Trust me, it will be a blood bath if we march into town and forcibly take them from there. His daughter isn't ready and hasn't morphed yet, she'll probably try to kill us first. I know that Alpha will kill *us if we try to approach her or any one but him and his Beta. You know they won't leave until his daughter has morphed."* Cole says sternly his voice firm. Asher nods, *"I know, your right. It's just that, the pack is getting eager. Soon I won't be able to stop them. I'm not the real alpha; I'm only the standing Alpha. They're beginning to question my authority."* He says.

"That's going to be a problem then." A deep, familiar voice said. Both boys turn around, their eyes now showing silver. They drop their gazes to the floor.

"Alpha," Cole says, and then everything begins to fade.

~ ~ ~

I open my eyes, surprised to see a ceiling above me, and feel a comfy cushion under me. "Xander?" I ask slowly sitting up slowly, feeling my head spin and back ache. I put my hand on my forehead and realize my skin was burning hot even though I feel freezing. I wonder if I'm sick and why I keep feeling cold flashes. I turn my head and look right into the wide, surprised eyes of Lucy Uriel.

"Xander, she's awake!" she smiles as she shouts, jumping off her chair and running upstairs. Xander comes down shortly after with some beef stew. He smiles nervously as he hands me the stew carefully.

"How are you feeling?" he asks quietly, sitting next to me.

"Not too good." I reply taking a bite of stew. "But better off than if a bunch of Dreads had ripped me to pieces… Thanks for saving me, again." I add with a slight smile that vanishes instantly when I remember what he is- a half Dread. His smile disappears as well and he pushes his hand through his now longer, dark, wavy hair nervously. He still hasn't cut it since he got back from the forest; his stubble is still growing out. His eyes darken and he looks at the floor.

"So what do you plan on doing to me now that you know?" He asks seriously, looking back into my eyes, his golden eyes sparkle with innocence and pain. My stomach flops inside me and I feel unsure all of the sudden. *What am I supposed to do about him?* I wonder.

"Well, you haven't hurt anyone yet. And you seem to have really good control of that monster side of you. I think that you aren't guilty of being a monster so I cannot kill you and neither can my father. If that changes then I will have a responsibility to do my duty. So, don't harm or kill anyone and then I can't harm or kill you. Does that sound like a good agreement?" I say slowly, thinking carefully before answering. He nods and says nothing after for a while.

"I'm glad you're okay. You gave me a big scare back in the forest. Your whole body got extremely warm and you weren't breathing right, you started hyperventilating. I knew something was wrong but I couldn't figure out what it was, not even my parents or your mother." He says shaking his head.

"My mother's here?" I ask looking at the door that leads to the upstairs.

"Yeah, she's just chatting with my mom." He replies standing up. I stay where I am unsure of what to do next. "I know that you're afraid of me. I can smell it." He says looking at me with hard golden eyes.

"I'm not afraid of you." I say looking away knowing I'm lying. I don't know what to expect from Xander now, but he is my friend and I know he won't hurt me on purpose. I care about him and don't want to hurt him because of what Nicki did to him. He turns away, his fists clenched.

"You're lying…" He sighs, "I get it. You don't trust me, that's fine. I understand why. Sometimes I don't even trust myself." he looks at the floor, then at his clenched fist. He relaxes his hand and lets it fall to his side, his nails are claws. He takes a deep breath and then releases it and the claws retract back to nails. *He really does have control.* I think in amazement, standing up and putting my hand on his shoulder. All of my fear melts away and I know that I don't need to be for now. He turns to me in surprise; a small smile grows on my face that he returns slightly.

"Half monster or not we are friends, and I stick with my friends through thick and thin. It isn't your fault Nicki bit you." I say remembering Kyle's fate. "I'm not going to leave you to suffer through this alone." I look into his eyes.

"Thank you." he whispers quietly. I hear footsteps coming down the stairs and drop my hand off Xander's shoulder. My mother and Mrs.Uriel come through the door.

"Oh Anika, I'm so glad you're awake." my mother says hugging me tightly, I hug her back. "Come on, let's go home." We thank the Uriels for taking care of me and calling my mother then we go home.

"They explained to me what happened. I know what Xander is, he showed me." My mother says sitting down with me on our couch with some hot cocoa.

"I just found out today."

"Anika, that boy is dangerous. He is going to kill someone. It may be an accident but it's going to happen. You have a responsibility to this town, that boy can't live much longer. You understand that right?" My mother says pushing her wavy brown hair behind her ear before taking a sip of her cocoa.

"Yes mother, I made it clear that it is what I have to do if anything happens. It's my responsibility as a hunter to so."

"I want you to carry your dagger and Kyle's old dagger with you at all times, just in case." She looks at me seriously.

"Yes mother, I always do."

"Good, I just want you safe. And our family has never been safe. Please watch out for yourself will you?" I nod. My mother smiles and takes another sip. She wants me to keep an eye on Xander, and that will require me to watch him at all times.

~ ~ ~

The weekend goes by without anything interesting happening and I begin to feel more aware of the dreams I've been having. October eleventh is getting closer and closer, only four more weeks. I shiver; something big is going to happen that day. I can feel it in my bones.

I walk around school with Melanie and Lani who seems to be doing a lot better lately. We talk about how this Friday was my half birthday and that even though it's only my half birthday, we should celebrate it. That's when we all see it. Posted on every door in school is a flier that doesn't make any sense. We all stare in shock.

"Did you guys know about this?" Melanie asks,

"Yeah but, I thought they were rumors." Lani answers. The flier is an announcing that Homecoming, both the game and the Dance are this Friday. This is odd because Wolfsbane High never has Dances or Home football games because of the Dreads. The flier states that the dance theme is a Masquerade Ball. Something feels wrong about it.

"Why on earth would we have Homecoming this year of all years? It's the most dangerous year we've had with Dreads. It makes no sense." I say taking down the flier and rolling it up to take home and show my mother.

"Yes, but… It's a dance! We've never had one before! If I get asked, I'm totally going!" Melanie giggles. Lani and I shake our heads.

"I'm not going. Something doesn't feel right about it. Anika has a point. It makes no sense." Lani says pushing through the Cafeteria doors to get her lunch, we follow her in.

When I get home after school I show my mother the school dance flier and she is puzzled by it as well. I tell her that I lost my bow in the forest and she give me a hand gun with several copper bullets and tells me to be careful and to see if Jackson will help me find it.

I can't find Jackson; I assume he went with my hunting with my father. So I end up jogging to the edge of the forest alone. I hesitate before entering the woods, remembering what things lie in wait to kill me hidden by the trunks. I scan the trees feeling uneasy. I listen for a long time and then enter the forest deciding to find my bow as quickly as I can. I pull out my dagger, feeling the family crest imbedded in its hilt.

My father had given me this copper dagger when I was eight. That's when I first started training to be a hunter, when I first picked up Archery. I suddenly feel a burst of courage and stride into the forest determined to find my bow. I walk cautiously, yet alert and feel in total control.

I look for what feels like hours but has only been about fifteen minutes. My bow is nowhere to be found. There are a couple times I think I have seen a shadow or an outline of a figure near by but I think my mind is playing tricks on me. I look for five more minutes and start getting frustrated. I can't find it anywhere.

I look at my wristwatch, checking the time. It's three thirty. I've been looking for forty five minutes now. I sigh and shove sweater sleeve over my watch telling myself that in five more minutes if I don't find my bow I'm going home.

That's when I hear a twig snap not too far from me. It startles me and I glance behind me to see a shadow duck behind a tree a few feet away from me. I sprint back toward the town line, panic rises inside me. I glance behind me to see the figure chasing me, and it's gaining. I look forward and take a right turn suddenly and run faster. I make the mistake of turning around again to see if the shadow has followed me when I trip over a fallen log.

I fall on my back, knocking the wind out of my lungs. I know I'm toast now. I start to feel freezing and my arms and legs feel goose bumps begin to form again and I push myself off the ground. *Looks like I'll have to fight my way out of this.* I think bracing myself. The shadow leaps to a tree to my right, I start sprinting again. The shadow climbs up the tree and jumps from the trees, branch to branch. Next thing I know it jumps from the tree and lands gracefully on the ground in front of me. I skid to a stop, not believing my eyes.

"Whoa, Anika stop. It's okay, it's only me." Xander says. Pure terror is replaced with anger and annoyance.

"You scared the living daylights out of me!" I say through gritted teeth, pointing my copper dagger at him, glaring. He holds up his hands innocently and takes a step back.

"Hey, I was just watching over you. You know, just in case. Besides you're the one who went in the forest alone. I decided to follow you if you got into any trouble." he says smugly.

"How long have you followed me?" I ask lowering my dagger.

"When I saw you enter in the woods." He lowers his hands. "You're welcome." I hear his cocky side coming out; I roll my eyes in response.

"Thanks?" I reply walking past him. He follows me, keeping my pace.

"Are you looking for your bow?" he asks,

"Yes, I am."

He turns suddenly to a tree near by, and starts to climb it.

"Wait here." He commands. He disappears up the tree then comes down with something in his hand.

"Thank you." I breathe taking my bow from him feeling both surprised and relieved.

"Yep, you're welcome." He says, looking uneasy.

"What's wrong?" I ask.

"Nothing," He replies starting to walk. I grab his hand to stop him, he freezes in mid step.

"What's wrong?" I repeat.

"Homecoming."

"What about it?" I ask, Xander tries to leave again but I don't let go of his hand. "Please tell me."

"You should already know." He says smiling guiltily, I raise an eyebrow at him and he sighs.

"Homecoming consists of a football game, and… a dance." he says, wrapping his fingers around mine, looking at our interlocked hands.

"Yeah, it does." I state wondering why he'd say something so obvious and watch as our fingers entwine while a tingling feeling shoots through my hand and up my arm, I'm having difficulty breathing for some reason.

"And I was wondering… if you'd like to go… you know… with… me?"

I stare at him with my mouth agape. *Homecoming is the last thing on my mind, but a dance, with Xander? It seems so impossible.*

"If you don't want to go, you just had to say no." He says releasing my hand and turning on his heel.

"What? Are you kidding? I'd love to go!" I shout at him, surprising myself.

"So that's a yes?" He smiles turning back around to face me,

"Sure, yes, of course!" I smile back.

"Friday night?"

"Friday," I nod.

~ ~ ~

It is now Friday the twentieth of September, my half birthday, and the Homecoming game and dance. The game had ended hours ago at seven thirty. Nothing went wrong at the game except for the fact that it had started snowing, which makes me a little more relaxed about the dance tonight. I get ready in my dress that my mother made for me, a modest turquoise dress with a lace up back and short lacey sleeves. It has black swirls and flowers on the bodice and is form fitting, the skirt goes to the ground and fluffs slightly with a long train, like a princess dress. It's a beautiful gown and it compliments my skin tone. My hair is falling with curls that frame my face and pull back in a princess look with curls falling down my back. I feel beautiful. I have black high heels on, a black metal mask that has swirls that match my dress, and a small purse, and a black flower in my hair to pull it all together. My father just barely got home tonight and I'm glad that he'd get to see me off to the dance.

"Wow sweetheart, you look gorgeous." he says as he hugs me. I smile and hug him back. "Here, I want you to have this." he says putting something cold and metal in my hand. I open it to see my father's small pocket watch that he has put on a chain that is meant to be a necklace. The back has the family crest on it and the front has a carving of the moon. I click it open to see a picture of my family in it along with a small clock on the other side.

"Thank you father, it's beautiful." I say in awe. He puts it around my neck then hugs me again.

"Anika, always remember who you are. You're a Conall, the blood runs in your veins. Be strong. We always find strength when we least expect it. Be safe tonight, something about it feels wrong. I have a bad feeling but I trust you. Be careful and call if anything goes wrong. Do you have your dagger with you?" I nod, remembering it strapped to my leg under my dress. "Good, be ready for anything." I nod thinking, *I always am.*

~ ~ ~

My father drives me to the dance feeling uneasy which doesn't help my feelings either, apparently my father had called Xander and told him to meet me at the dance so my father could take me. My father has never gone through the whole dance thing; none of the people here have, so we are just going with the flow. I'm not sure what to expect when I get there, I nervously open and close my new watch. My father pulls up in the parking lot and escorts me to the Gymnasium doors. "I'm going to be patrolling the school grounds and checking in every once in a while at the dance. Have fun, if you run into any trouble come find me." My father says, and hugs me one last time before opening the door for me. I thank him and walk inside the gym.

It is surprisingly full on the dance floor. I didn't think that many kids went to Wolfsbane High but maybe I'm mistaken. The gym is wonderfully decorated with red and black streamers, balloons, and lights. I guess that Dana is trying to do her best in Nicki's place as student body president since the head cheer leader's disappearance. The DJ from out of town is set up at the opposite end of the gym with lights moving rapidly over the dance floor giving it a club like feel. The punch table is in the corner near the back where I find Xander standing with one hand in his pocket, the other holding a glass of punch. He watches the people dancing, waiting for me. He looks very handsome in a suit and black tie. He combs and gels his hair which he had cut to the length it had been when he first moved in and he doesn't wear a mask like everyone else does. I smile knowing what a lucky girl I am, having the nicest, most attractive guy in Wolfsbane as my date. Girls flock to him, strutting around him, practically begging him for his attention. When his eyes meet mine, he stands in awe looking dumb founded, making me blush. He can't seem look away and doesn't notice the other girls now practically throwing themselves at him. We start walking toward each other when someone stops in front of me, blocking my view of Xander. I look up to meet Marcus' dark brown eyes. He smirks over confidently down at me. "What's a beautiful young damsel such as yourself doing at the Homecoming dance without a date?" he asks mischievously.

"Well actually I do have-" I start to say but Marcus cuts me off,

"I'll be the polite young man and dance with the lonely young woman." he grabs my hand and pulls me to the dance floor. I try to escape but Marcus is too strong.

"Marcus, I have a date and I'm sure you have one too, now please let go and find the girl you asked." I demand.

"I heard your Uriel's date, but he doesn't deserve you. He's nothing but a snake that one." Marcus sneers, twirling me at which point I try getting free but end up bumping into a near by couple who glare at me. "Careful now, you don't want to be a klutz. It's very unattractive." Marcus pulls me closer; I push against his chest defiantly.

"Excuse me but I do believe the young lady already has a date. Which happens to be me, mind if I cut in?" A deep, familiar voice asks, butterflies explode in my stomach at the sound of his voice.

"Xander, thank goodness." I say taking Xander's hand and he pulls me free of Marcus' grasp while looking into Marcus' eyes as if challenging him.

"This isn't over Uriel." Marcus say through clenched teeth, and turns on his heel, disappearing into the dancing crowd of masks, suits, and dresses.

"Thank you for saving me." I say smiling at him.

"How could I not? A beautiful damsel in distress calls for a hero." He winks, smiling. "You really do look amazing Anika, but you don't need the mask." He admits, I blush hoping it is too dark for him to notice but keep my mask on, feeling as though it is protection shielding my growing feelings for him. A slow song starts and he pulls me closer to him but keeps a comfortable distance. Electricity buzzes through my body where our hands are connected and with his hand at the small of my back. I can't look anywhere but in his perfect golden eyes, and smile like an idiot. We dance to the beat of the music, slowly swaying. I feel my whole body start to get freezing toward the end of the song, goose bumps appear on my arms and legs soon, and start to feel dizzy. *No one has ever affected me like this before…* I think, and to my surprise Xander's smile disappears and a look of concern appears on his face.

"Anika, you're burning up. Are you feeling okay?" he asks. *But I feel freezing…* I think to myself suddenly feeling sick. I shake my head, he take my hand and leads me to a seat near the exit of the gym and has me sit down. "Wait here, I'm going to get you a drink and if you want I can take you home." He says sadly. I shake my head.

"No, I'll be fine, just a drink sounds fine thank you." I say not wanting to go home and end this perfect night with him yet. He nods, concern etched on his face and hurries toward the punch table. I see Melanie and her date Cedric dancing near the DJ table; they look like they were having fun. I feel an angry feeling in the pit of my stomach, jealously. I wish I didn't feel sick so Xander and I can be having that much fun.

I look over at the punch table at Xander who is being mauled by crazy girls. I feel a huge pang of jealousy and decide that I need some fresh air. My feet are starting to hurt from walking in heels so much and I feel like I am going to barf. Before walking out the door, I turn and look at Xander who is still surrounded by girls. I roll my eyes and turn my attention to the other people dancing and realize I don't recognize over half of them.

That's strange, isn't this a school dance? I think, and that's when I realize it: they aren't all high school students. Some of them are Dreads- their muscular bodies, cruel eyes and jagged movements. I wonder why I don't notice before. Then I realize that Xander have done what I told myself I wouldn't allow him to do. He distracted me, made me feel so safe that I let my guard down... and walked right into a huge trap. Several fancy dressed Dreads turn and look at me, smirking as if they were waiting for me to notice their true identities.

    I turn and push open the emergency exit door, and run dizzily toward the football field's parking lot. I have to find my father, but I'm not alone- I am followed by four huge Dread guys. I try running faster but my heels, the slippery snow, and dizziness aren't helping me at all. I stumble and fall to the ice cold ground. Instinctively, I reach for my dagger but it's knocked out of my hand. They grab me and bind my hands. One flings me over their shoulder like a rag doll. I try screaming but am knocked out by one of the Dreads. The last thing I remember is hearing Xander's voice calling out for me.

Chapter 16: Homecoming
-Xander

I go to get Anika a glass of fruit punch when I am suddenly surrounded by girls. Well, not normal girls- Dread girls. By then I have noticed the whole gym is infested with Dreads. I have to get away. I have to warn Anika, I look around for her but she isn't in the seat where I had left her. I look toward the doors to see her turn and practically run out of them, followed by four big, burley looking Dreads. I fight against the girl Dreads, unsure whether or not to hit them. My mother had taught me to never hit girls but she never said anything about monster girls. I eventually manage to escape the horde of girl Dreads that are guarding me.

I sprint out the door and see them pick her up off the snow covered ground and throw her over on of their shoulders. "Anika!" I yell running at them. "Let her go!" I demand charging at them faster. They are ready for me. My anger transforms me into the half Dread and I jump toward the first Dread, giving him a round house kick to the face. He stumbles back shaking his head to rid the pain. I go at him again, swiping my leg under both of his making him collapse to the ground. I pounce on him, grabbing his leg and bending it a way it should never be able to go, I hear a cracking sound and he roars in pain. The other two charge at me and the one that carries a now unconscious Anika runs into the forest. Before the two get to me, I slam the head of the Dread I am fighting into a rock, his whole body goes limp.

Suddenly chaos breaks out and there is screaming coming from the gym, the doors burst open and Dreads are carrying nicely dressed teens out under their arms and running into the forest just like they did with Anika. The girls scream, the guys yell and try to fight their way out but it is no use.

I am so distracted by this that I am grabbed from behind before I can dodge. I turn and punch the face of the Dread that grabbed me and slap his ears with both of my hands making his ears ring, he staggers away. I don't see the third one in time. He grabs my legs and swings me in the air, then releases me. I hit the side of the school hard and collapse. They are taking revenge on me for killing their comrade. They throw me around a couple more times; weakening me to the point I can't fight it anymore. They shred my suit and tie and I am bleeding profusely from my wounds. "Now look what you did, this is my best suit." I spit lying helpless on the ground. I feel a stinging pain in my head and Nicki's voice fills my thoughts.

You should have joined us, now Anika and all of your class mates will pay dearly for your mistake. She hisses in my head. I groan as I look up to see both of the Dreads smiling cruelly, enjoying my pain. One of them raises its arm, ready to slit my throat when I hear two gun shots to my right some where. The two Dreads fall instantly, dead with their blood smeared across the snow. Everything starts to go fuzzy; the last thing I see is Anika's father standing above me pointing his gun at my head.

~ ~ ~

When I come to, it is still dark and I find my brother and Lani standing over me worriedly holding flashlights.

"Xander, good you're finally awake." Lani says looking relieved.

"What happened here?" Mason asks looking at the school. I sit up and mumble something that sounds like 'chaos'. I look around for Deputy Conall but he is no where in sight. I notice we are under the bleachers.

"How'd we get under the bleachers?" I ask slowly getting to my feet.

"We found you lying unconscious under here." Lani says.

"Mom and dad are so worried when you never showed up after the dance was supposed to end. They thought you disappeared again. The police got calls from people that said they heard screaming coming from the school and more calls that teens weren't coming home. The police went to check out the scene and found no one, the dance was completely deserted but it did look like something happened. Xander, every teen that went to that dance is missing, except for you." Mason explains. That's when it all comes back to me, the fighting, the people screaming, the Dreads, and Anika.

"I remember..." I whisper, walking to the school building, having flash backs.

"Remember what?" Mason demands.

"Dreads, everywhere, they grabbed everyone here and took them into the forest. I was fighting them but... I lost." I say bitterly.

"Obviously," Lani say looking at my shredded suit.

"They took Anika too, I couldn't save her, there were too many of them." I say feeling guilty inside. I know if anything happened to her, it will be my fault.

"Are you bleeding?" Lani ask, looking at the blood on my suit.

"I was, I heal faster than normal. I'm guessing you've figured out what happened to me." I reply walking ahead of them to the gym doors.

"Yeah, Mason told me." was all she says. I push open the door and look inside. The gym was dark. I flick on the lights and walk inside followed by Mason and Lani. The streamers are all over the floor; the balloons are either popped littering the floor or floating near the ceiling. The punch was spilled all over the floor and the plastic cups were stepped on. Chairs litter the floor lying sideways, the DJ table is split in half and the equipment in pieces on the floor.

"They took every teen but harmed none of them, how strange." Lani says, side stepping fallen chairs and spilled punch. I can smell bitter soap in the air, the smell of fear, but it isn't coming from Mason or Lani. Someone else is still in the building. I follow the scent into the hallway which is dark. It is coming from the men's restroom. Mason and Lani stop in front of it seeing that I am staring at it.

"What is it?" Mason asks sniffing the air. Fear wasn't the only putrid smell that radiates from the room; we all eye the door to the restroom.

"There's someone in there." I replies pushing on the door to open it, something is blocking. I push harder, the scent getting more potent. "Help me." I push harder, they help and we push it open enough to squeeze through one at a time. I turn on the light and see that someone has killed a huge Dread and pressed it up against the door to block it from other people entering. I push the lifeless Dread body away from the door and follow the scent to the last stall. I kick it open and am surprised to find Marcus backed against the wall. His suit is covered in red punch and his hair is ruffled and crazy, his eyes look like a scared, angry, desperate animal. When he realizes it's me he runs at me with a copper dagger in his hand. I hit his wrist, grab him by the throat, and pin him against a wall.

"Calm down Marcus, we're here to help you." Lani says picking up the dagger and studying it. "This is Anika's dagger, where did you find it?" she demands. Marcus spits at me.

"You're not here to help me. You're here to take me to them." He growls glaring at me, hatred boils in his eyes.

"What are you talking about?" I demand,

"You're one of them. I know it. You let them take Anika and everyone else, I saw. They would have taken me too if I hadn't found that dagger on the ground. One of them chased me in here and I stabbed it and it fell against the door, I hid in the stall waiting for others like you." He sneers.

"I wouldn't let them take her! Or anyone, I tried fighting them off, but…" I stop myself.

"You got your butt kicked didn't you?" He grins, "I know you're one of them, but even they enjoy kicking your butt. Anika is probably already dead or one of them same as our school mates. And that's all because of you." Marcus spits. The comment makes rage explode within me. I start to change into the Dread form, I can feel it. His eyes widen in fear and my grip on his neck tightens, he gasps.

"Don't you dare say that! If they hurt her, or any of them, they will pay for that mistake." I growl. His face starts turning blue and I release him watching him sag to the floor coughing for oxygen. I take a deep breath to calm myself down, returning back to normal. "Get him home, he needs some rest. I have somewhere I need to go. I'm getting all of them back, tonight." I say without looking at them, I walk out of the restroom knowing there is only one person that can help me now.

Chapter 17: Prisoner

-Anika

I can't breathe or see anything. I cough feeling shackles on my wrists and ankles the chains holding me down to the floor. I hear crying and whispering nearby. I groan feeling sick and cold. My whole body is shivering and I have a pounding headache. My mind is reeling with questions that no one could answer. I wonder what happened to Xander and who else is down here with me. Where I am, what is going to happen to me, and why I feel so sick. I whimper feeling pain everywhere, in my jaw, my gums, my legs, my arms, my back and my veins. Ice courses through them making each breath and heart beat spike the pain.

"Anika? Is that you? I can't see anything." a familiar voice asks. I slowly open my eyes to see a couple of candles dimly lit the room enough for me to see several figures behind bars. The one who spoke is watching me with her hands gripping the bars. From the voice I guess it's Melanie. I groan again in response, unable to find my voice. "Anika? What's wrong, you've been shivering since we got here. Are you okay?" She sounds worried, I want to comfort her but my head is all fuzzy and everything hurts. "I'm scared; they keep coming in and taking us two at a time. They don't tell us anything, or even speak. What do they want with us?" Her voice quivers. I hear a door open and footsteps.

"That one," I hear Nicki say. I turn to see her pointing at Melanie. The two Dreads grab Melanie who screams and they pull her out of the room. Nicki approaches me and bends down and looks at me with a sense of accomplishment. "You're time will be soon. Oh revenge is sweet." She laughs, I growl at her. "Oh, see it's almost time. At last I can finally rid this world of my natural enemy." She stands up and walks from the room, "See you soon." She says smiling before the door closes behind her. I growl again, filled with rage. I stand up and try to move but the chains don't let me move more than one step each way. I want to scream but I can't for some reason. *What's wrong with me!* I scream in my head. I wait for Nicki to come back but she doesn't. About ten minutes later I hear gears turning, I feel the floor under me moving. The ceiling is getting closer to me. Just before my head is going to hit it, the ceiling opens revealing bright lights and deafening noise. I squint holding my hands over my ears. When my eyes adjust I realize I am on a stage. The ground under me shakes to a stop, almost knocking me over. I feel weak and threatened, the crowd is huge and is made of all Dreads, and there are hundreds of them. I look on the stage and see four teens, Melanie included, tied down on their knees on stage. Growls, shouts, and the sound of drums are deafening from the audience. My headache grows worse and the shackles on me are burning my wrists. I notice they are made of pure silver. I turn to see Nicki walk onto the stage and the cheering gets louder.

"At long last, we have our revenge!" Nicki shouts making the crowd go even crazier. "We have the town's precious children who forced us away to live like animals in these woods so many years ago! And now we have a Slayer who has hunted and killed us for centuries!" She announces, I look around and don't see a Slayer anywhere. "The time has come to kill the Alpha and his Pack!" She roars tearing my black mask off my face and then pumping her fist in the air and pointing at the ceiling. I look where she's pointing to see that there's a huge hole in the roof and the ceiling exposing the sky, the moonlight begins to flow down through it. I feel entranced, and then a horrifying burning pain bursts through me. I howl out in pain like a blood thirsty beast, finally finding my voice. I look down at my hands panicking. Copper claws grow where my fingernails were, my legs give out and I fall to my knees, my eyes widen. *What's happening?* I scream in my head, clawing at the wooden stage. Pain surges through me again, my ears and nose extend and suddenly there is a snout with brown fur, I feel my jaw ache and canines rip through my gums. My spine cracks painfully and I howl again, and everything is fuzzy. I hear something rip; I guess it's my dress. That makes me grateful that I'm wearing a tank top and black leggings under it. Something is definitely wrong, what have they done to me?

Chapter 18: Enemy
-Xander

After running home to change from my nice dress clothes into jeans, a gray t-shirt, my black Nikes, and my favorite dark blue hoodie, I knock on the Conall's door to be welcomed by a copper machete pressed against my throat. "If you want to live you will tell me where they've taken my daughter." Deputy Conall says glaring.

"I don't know where they took her. But I'm going to get her back. I need your help to do that. You know more about them than I do. Please, help me." I plead.

"Why should I help you? How can I trust you? I know you're one of them. I can smell it," He says, scrunching his nose in disgust, "they probably sent you here to throw me off. Why would you even care about saving her?" he asks fiercely taking a step closer to me pushing the blade against my skin. "Why shouldn't I kill you right here and now?"

"Because I love her, I will do anything to get her back safely." I state, my voice unwavering. My words surprise even me, but I mean them. Her father looks shocked at my declaration, but he knows I'm not kidding. He lowers his weapon and pulls me inside his home and slamming the door and locking it behind me. I follow him to his study. He went to one end and punch in numbers on a keypad. The wall slides open revealing a huge armory filled and stocked with weapons.

"So you said you can smell that I'm part Dread, how?" I ask curiously. The Deputy raises his eyebrow in surprise.

"You really don't know much of Dread history do you?" He asks turning to a bookshelf and picking up a book.

"I don't know much about any of this,"

"Well, you know there are opposites of everything, right? Such as: black and white, wet and dry, good and evil?" He says opening the book, I nod. "Well, in all legends, creatures always have an opposite."

"Like Werewolves and Vampires?"

"Yes, exactly like that." He replies flipping through pages.

"So that must mean… Dreads have a natural enemy." I say catching on,

"Precisely,"

"What is their natural enemy?"

Deputy Conall looks at me mischievously. I notice that his irises in his eyes are now silver, and he smiles, revealing canine like fangs. I back away from him, the monster part in me feels defensive and is trying to take over, and I fight for control. He walks past me and sets the book on his desk and slides it across so I can see its contents. The page he has opened up to has the title 'Slayer' at the top, the picture looks like a werewolf but it's more giant and wolf-like than man like. I recognize it from that night I was chased by three of them in the forest when I was missing. I shiver from the memory.

"A Slayer," I state, staring at the page.

"Yes, a Dread's worst nightmare. I'm the Alpha of the Pack that is stationed here. It runs in my bloodline, Sheriff Darwin is my strongest Beta and he is here with me. The rest of my Pack is somewhere in the woods." He explains,

"Yeah, I think I've met some of them." I say closing the book.

"Slayers are cousins to Werewolves but have been appointed by the Moon to balance the evil creatures that only kill to kill. We, like Werewolves, are strongest during a full moon."

"You said it runs in your blood line, does that mean that-"

"Yes, Anika is also a Slayer. Well, kind of."

"Kind of?"

"She doesn't exactly know it runs in our bloodline. And she hasn't turned yet, but I have a feeling she will at some point tonight. We need to find her quickly before she does. She won't know her own strength or how to control herself and she'll be too frightened to understand what's happening. The Dreads know that the first transformation is when a Slayer is most vulnerable. They will take advantage of that." He says his silver eyes filled with anger and worry. He strides over to his armory and grabs a large duffle bag and start filling it with weapons.

"Why hasn't she turned before?"

"Every Slayer's first Morph is different, but the Moon has told me that Anika would turn when she was Seventeen and a half, today is her half birthday." He says as stuffing the bag with weapons.

"The Moon told you?" I think he is going a little crazy.

"Yes, the Moon told me. The Moon can tell the future. The Moon can also tell what's in your heart. The Moon only talks to the Alpha of the pack, which the Moon chooses. The Moon also connects the pack and helps them communicate when they are too far away to hear growling. The Moon also gives us the emotion of each Slayer when we are in that form." Deputy Conall is interrupted by a howl coming from the forest. It echoes across the trees, his eyes widen in panic. He looks at me and then starts packing faster then zips up the bag and tossing it at me effortlessly. "That was Anika, she's morphed." He says as he slings Anika's bow and her arrow over his shoulder and runs up the stairs; I follow him carrying the heavy bag of artillery behind him.

"If you're going to find her, I'm coming with you." I say, he nod apparently knowing I will go whether he wants me to or not.

"There are some things you should know that you probably haven't learned yet. Dreads are kind of like wolves. They like to travel in packs called Clans, the bigger the better. The Devilin is the Clan leader. He has Warriors that do his dirty work. Each Dread that becomes a Warrior is either the Devilin's offspring or the Devilin bit or sired them himself, and each has venom of the Dread which can turn human hosts into Dreads that don't have the venom. The Dread Warrior then has telepathic control over those it bites, laying claim to the Host. The Hosts do their Warrior's biding and share one mind when under the Warrior's control."

"So that's why I can hear Nicki's voice in my head." I say, he nods.

"If you kill the Warrior, you release the Host's minds that it controls. The Warriors can control their host's from far away, so not many Warriors can be killed." He explains, loading the truck bed of a black Dodge Ram. I set the artillery bag in the back of it as well. "There is one thing I don't understand," He says stopping at his garage door opener in the truck.

"What's that?"

"You, you're only half Dread. You were bitten but you didn't turn into one and they can't control you. How is that possible?"

"Nicki bit me during her transformation, she wasn't pure Dread yet. Do you think that's why?" I ask, he hands me Anika's bow and arrows and shakes his head.

"I think it may have to do with your strong will. You don't like to be bossed around do you?" I shake my head and he smirks, "There is one other thing, the Dread Warrior cannot function properly when one of the marked Hosts isn't mentally allied with them, their grip on the other Hosts weakens. They won't stop until they can have full control. That can only happen if the one that doesn't join them either changes their mind, or dies. They will come for you, and they won't stop until you're destroyed." Deputy Conall's eyes are serious, and now I understand why Nicki needs me dead so badly. He pushes the garage button and the garage open revealing the whole town holding flashlights and guns, pitch forks and shovels- Deputy Conall's eyes widen in surprise at this.

Mayor Rune steps out from among the crowd, his face completely blank, but a sinister look in his eyes. "Good evening, Clause, what brings you to my home along with the whole town?" Deputy Conall asks politely with a pit of acid in his tone.

"That's *Mayor Rune* to you Deputy Conall." The Mayor retorts in a tight voice. "We've come for the Uriel boy, Alexander. As we can all see, he is here with you, now hand him over." The Mayor demands. Deputy Conall steps in front of me protectively.

"Why do you want him? He's done nothing."

Mayor Rune's black eyes flicker from mine to the Deputy's. "It doesn't matter the reason. Hand him over, that is a direct order." The Mayor says in a stone cold voice. The Deputy doesn't move and inch. The town's people behind the Mayor are getting restless, men start shouting and glaring, women yell about how it's my fault their children were taken, and I know it was. Nicki has made that clear in my head.

My family was in the back but they were tied up and being guarded by town's people. "Citizen's of Wolfsbane! Our children have been abducted and possibly killed by those awful creatures that have plagued our wonderful town for centuries. This boy is one of them! I say we take him and show those horrid monsters that we will not just stand here and be bullied. Who's with me?" He ended his speech and the mass crowd of people cheered and charged into the Conall's garage, the Deputy grabbed my arm and ran into his house locking the door and ran out the back door.

"We've got to lose them in the woods! Follow me!" He commands and transforms as we hit the line separating the town from the woods. I allow my fear to transform me so I can keep up with the Slayer who is ironically saving my life. Conall gives out a loud, long howl into the night and keeps running, the howl is later returned by several other ones that sound far away. We came upon a clearing in the forest and stop, Conall sniffs the air. That's when he turns back into a human and looks at me seriously. "I don't know where Anika is unless she howls again. We'll wait here until my pack tells me more information." He says but right as he said it, it is too late. I feel a sudden burst of electricity enter my veins. The shock runs through me paralyzing every muscle. I drop to the ground like a rock. The same thing happens with Deputy Conall. A young man, about the age of twenty, emerges from the forest and the Sheriff does as well. The Sheriff bends down and binds me with copper wire on my wrists and ankles.

"Darwin? What are you doing! Tell Jackson to stop electrocuting me and free the boy. That is an order from your Alpha!" the Deputy shouts, gritting his teeth.

"I'm sorry Alpha. But I have to do this- for Kyle. They turned him into that thing. The Mayor is right. It's time we send them a message." Sheriff Darwin says gruffly pulling me up by the collar of my shirt.

"This is a mistake Darwin! That snake is a manipulative liar! If you do this you will never forgive yourself. Please Collin, just think for a moment!" Deputy Conall begs, but the only thing Sheriff Darwin does is take the bow and arrows from my still, tense body. By now the angry town's people have caught up to us. They tie me to a tree with copper wire that cuts into my skin and prevents my wounds from heeling and holds a copper dagger, they must have found in the back of the truck in the Conall's garage, to my neck.

They are going to kill me, and Nicki is going to get what she wants. My fate is set, I only hope that somehow fate will change its mind and intervene.

~ ~ ~

The whole town waits, hearing nothing. The Mayor stands out in front of them; he'd been talking to the forest for about thirty minutes now. Yelling at the Dreads to come and make a deal with him. I hope by now everyone is starting to see that he is crazy, but no one makes a move to stop or question him. I want to say something but every time I speak, the copper blade is pushed on my throat. Soon I notice my head is starting to hurt. Nicki's voice appears in my head. *Oh look, the one that got away came crawling back, oh and you brought some snacks with you, how generous.* She laughs in my head, I growl through my teeth, knowing exactly where she is. She comes out of the fog in front of us in the midst of the trees. The whole town gasps to see that she is half Dread. Even the Mayor is shocked.

"Nicki?" He asks in disbelief, she smiles cruelly at him.

"Hello father, and I see the town has come for a visit as well, how sweet." She says folding her arms, her Dread Hosts emerge from the fog behind her slowly some on all fours, others standing, growling and baring their fangs as they appear. Two of the biggest ones each hold a silver chain and a brown furred Slayer that looks like a larger wolf version of Darla has a silver collar around its neck is whimpering as they drag it on the ground next to Nicki. The sight tugs at my broken heart reopening my wounds of losing my dog, which makes me even angrier with Nicki.

"No," Deputy Conall lunges forward, only to be tazed again by the Sheriff's oldest son, and fall to the forest floor. I now realize that the light brown Slayer is Anika, and the collar is hurting her.

"Why have you all foolishly come out in the forest?" Nicki asks,

"We have come to show we will not be bullied by you monsters anymore."

"Is that so? And what is to stop us from killing you all right now?"

"We have something you want." The mayor points at me, Nicki smiles.

"Actually you have three things we want."

"Three? What are the other things?" Sheriff Darwin demands, Nicki points at the Sheriff and the Deputy.

"Them."

"What? Why?" the Sheriff demands,

"What business is it of yours? Just hand them over."

"In exchange we want our teenagers back." The Mayor says, the crowd of people gasp and whisper, giving up the Sheriff and Deputy meant giving up their protection against the Dreads, soon no one would be safe, but Mayor Run doesn't seem to care.

"You will get nothing, except a few minutes to get a head start back to town before we kill you." She growls. *What a brat* I think to myself.

"We accept your terms." the Mayor states to everyone's surprise and turns to the people. The people whisper unhappily and frightened. The Mayor motions for them to bring me over along with the Sheriff and the Deputy.

"Oh, and, we want Kyle too." She says smiling.

"We don't have Kyle. You do!" the Sheriff spits. Nicki smiles mischievously.

"What a shame." She says, pausing as she watches the Sheriff, challenging him. The town holds their breath. She turns to wolf Anika revealing a silver knife in her hands. Both the sheriff and the deputy stiffen at the blade. She tosses it around effortlessly watching them flinch when she catches it. "I don't have Kyle, if you're hiding him, you'll regret it." she says, and she raises the blade threateningly at Anika. "No!" Deputy Conall yells and she waits. "Where is he?" Nicki demands, no one answers. "Bring him to me!." she shouts. No one moves, "Fine," she whispers, and turns stabbing Anika in the side of her rib cage in one fluid motion, wolf Anika yelps falling down and convulsing on the ground until she appears human again-dressed in a black tank top and leggings. She lay on the ground, bleeding and unconscious. Nicki growls, the Dreads begin to advance, Sheriff Darwin drops Anika's bow and arrows and transformed into a Slayer, same as his son and Deputy Conall. The town's people are frightened and surprised by this run away in fear. It's all chaos. Deputy Conall howls a deep, long howl and slices my copper bindings with his huge copper claws. I rub my wrists but transform as well, ready to rip Nicki's head off. I tackle her, hissing and blind with anger.

"You will pay for that, for everything you've done! For every innocent person you have poisoned with your bite!" I growl, the monster part of me taking over. I scratch her face with my claws, she groans in pain and pushes me off her so hard and fast I fly through the air and hit a nearby tree. A few Dreads jump me and knock some sense into me. I realize that we are totally out numbered. There are hundreds of Dreads and only three Slayers and one me.

We won't be able to fight off all of them. I need to get rid of Nicki, and then it would destroy her connection and control of her Hosts. I'm getting my butt handed to me- the Dreads tare at me. I fight back twice as hard. I strangely don't feel any of their blows or cuts; I'm numb whenever I catch a glimpse of Anika's still body lying helplessly on the ground.

Eventually I find my way to Nicki who is battling the gray Slayer- Deputy Conall. She has in her hand the silver knife, trying to stab the Alpha. He claws at her, dodging the blade, I knock it out of her hands and hold her to the ground. I pick up the knife and hold it to her throat, she laughs. "You should know better, Silver doesn't kill Dreads."

I look at the knife and shrug and stuck it in my back pocket. "Looks like I'll have to find some copper then." I say glairing. She smiles innocently, that's when I'm knocked off her by a huge hand, and I feel something crack in my chest. I push myself up, my blood pounding already fixing my broken bone. I turn over and see a huge, eight foot tall Dread standing over my head. It's pale, hugely muscular, and has scale covered skin like a snake or lizard. Its fangs are huge and it has black hair pulled back into a well groomed pony tale. It reminds me of a giant Lord Voldemort from Harry Potter, with scales all over, black hair, and pure black eyes. That's when it hits me; it's the Devilin, the Dread Leader in the flesh. Not only is he the Devilin, but also the town's very own Mayor. His cold black eyes and pony tail are what give it away. "I can see the resemblance. You are the spitting image of your father Nicki, pure monster." I snarl. She bared her teeth at me and roared with anger; her father grabbed me by the collar of my shirt.

"Don't talk to my daughter you fool! You betray your own kind- and for what -a stupid girl, a family that fears you, a town who wants to kill you?" Mayor Rune roars and punched me, sending me flying into a tree, breaking it in half. "You will regret your stupidity." He laughs, for once I am grateful for my Dread side- it saves me more than I give it credit for. The Devilin then turns to Alpha Conall. They begin to battle it out. That left me to a bunch of blood thirsty Dreads. Jackson and Sheriff Darwin are both fighting Nicki, who is clever at evading their attacks. I am bombarded by Dreads; I need to find some copper. I saw several people drop weapons as they ran off. I fight and search the ground. I find a gun that holds copper bullets and a copper dagger that happened to be lying next to it. I use the gun first, shooting at any Dreads that get too close. I try to aim for Nicki, but the Slayers keep blocking me, or run in front of her, sacrificing themselves to keep her alive, I doubt they'd do that if they weren't under her control. I grow frustrated and notice that I have run out of bullets, I continue injuring, but not killing Dreads with the dagger.

    Once I cut them they fall instantly to the ground in shock. They aren't as strong when it comes to the copper metal. I hear a roar behind me to see that Alpha Conall is being twisted in Silver chains, stuck. I run to his aid and jump on the Devilin's back, stabbing him in the side. He roars, dropping the chains. He grabs me and throws me on the ground; the dagger falls from my hands.

"You don't understand boy. I can't die so easily. I am a purebred. You are a Mutt Host, or half of one. That means you are still weak and can die by the ways of a human, or a Dread," He grabs me by the throat and presses me up against a tree. "You are weak. You are nothing compared to me."

"That's not true is it? You need me, don't you? Nicki needs me. Or she will lose control of her Hosts. I'm more than you say I am. You may think I'm weak, but I am strong in both the ways of the Dreaded and a human. You know that, you're afraid of that!" I argue, he tightens his grip on my neck, reminding me of what I had done to Marcus not too long ago, *Wow; Karma really does always come back around.* I think to myself. Soon I begin to squirm, my lungs beg for air. Black dots invade my vision and I feel myself weaken. I know I'll black out soon; the darkness creeps into my vision from the outside in.

"You will not be my problem anymore." Mayor Rune growls. Then I'm released and I hear a loud roar, I drop to the ground landing on my butt feeling dizzy. I gasp, sucking in as much oxygen as my lungs will allow as I lean against a tree. The darkness from my vision fades and I start to see even though it's blurry. The Devilin has been scratched. Long, deep, bleeding claw marks cover his back. I shake my head to rid the dizziness and can feel my heart pounding in my head. I stand slowly to see he is fighting something.

    A brown Slayer, with an angry, hungered, vengeful look it its gleaming silver eyes. Anika is fighting. She's bleeding but somehow she is alive. She attacks the Devilin with full force, clawing, biting and growling. She is relentless and doesn't stop. Every time the Devilin throws or hits her she snaps back at him or lunges at him again. I stumble into Nicki. She has found that stupid silver knife that must have fallen from my pocket when her father grabbed me. She stabs Sheriff Darwin three times in the heart until he falls to the ground with a whimper and stops moving. She killed him; Jackson is furious at this and tackles Nicki with full force, snapping at her throat while her hosts come to her aid. I run around searching with something I can shoot long distance with. I remember Anika's bow and arrows. I recall Sheriff Darwin dropping them not too far from where the town's people had tied me to a tree.

I start there and look around when I come cross the couple of huge Dreads that had taken Anika into the forest earlier that night and had fought against me. They are Warriors just like Nicki which makes sense of why they are stronger and more competent than the Hosts. The biggest one holds up the bow, and the quiver. "Looking for these?" He sneers at me smiling big enough to show off his large fangs. My eyes narrow, I quickly come up with a plan, *I still have the copper dagger and even though it might not kill them right away, it would weaken them.* I think, near by I notice the copper wire I had been tied up with; I pick it up and run toward them. I knock two into a tree and tie the copper around them tightly, they fuss and complain.

"Burns doesn't it?" I ask tightening it and turning toward the next two. I take them down one by one and look around for the other one. The coward is running away from the fight with the bow and arrows. He is too far ahead for me to catch. I run after him anyway only to be tackled by a dirty blonde, unfamiliar Slayer. In surprise I push it off of me and pin it to a tree to be shocked by what it is. This Slayer, like me, is half Dread. I release it in shock. "Kyle?" The Slayer looks at me with confusion in its Dread eyes and then sniffs me. Kyle turns into his human form which is surprisingly full human.

"Xander? Why do you smell like the Dreaded?"

"I was bitten by one." I say showing the bite scar to him,

"Then why are you fighting against them? How are you not a full Host?" I shrug and then look at the Dread Warrior that is getting away with the weapons I need. Kyle follows my gaze. "Were you chasing him?"

"Yep, I need the bow and the arrows."

"I'm on it, oh and watch out. More Slayers are coming and they can't tell whose side you're on, your scent doesn't help distinguish it." He says turning away from me and leaping back into a Slayer-Dread and chasing after the Dread I was going for. He tackles it instantly and slices its throat with his copper ingrained claws. The Dread Warrior is defeated that instant. Kyle brings me the bow and arrows after that.

"Whoa, thanks man." I say taking the bow from him. He smiles and bows as if he has just done a fantastic performance. "Shall we get back to it?" He nods; we both turn and go back to the battle grounds. That's when the rest of the Slayer pack that Kyle had mentioned vaguely appears. There are tons of them. The one that seems to be leading them is a larger white Slayer with black fur on its chest. It sniffs the air and then lets out a loud growl. The rest of its huge pack descends into the chaos. Finally the battle seems even. I aim at a Dread just like I've seen Anika do and release the arrow, it hits the Dread in the shoulder and it falls instantly. I can't believe I hit it. "Yes! Boo-yah!" I shout and do a little victory dance. I open my eyes to see a group of confused looking

Dreads and two shocked Slayers watching me curiously.

I stop in mid-dance move and smile sheepishly. They then return to attacking each other and I am tackled by that white Slayer I had run from that night I escaped Nicki in the woods. It snarls at me and snaps his jaws at my throat. I grunt as I push it off me and stumble again losing the bow and the arrow attached to it. The rest of the arrows are still strapped to my back. I look around frantically only to be nearly crushed by the Devilin as he lands in front of me. Anika is growing weaker now. She collapses to the ground and again turns human, she is caked in blood and she looks unnaturally pale. The Devilin grabs me once again, squeezing my throat this time.

"And now I will finish you, without distractions." He sneers squeezing tighter and tighter. That's when a copper arrow launches into his heart. He drops me, again, and shock fills his dark eyes. He pulls the piercing copper arrow from his heart and drops it on the ground before falling himself. I whip my head around suddenly feeling less dizzy to see Anika standing with her bow in hand.

"Sorry, I am pretty distracting." She says, lowering her bow. She limps toward the Devilin's fallen figure with determination after putting her bow around her shoulder. The Dreads and Slayers stop in their tracks as they watch the scene unfold. Anika plucks a dagger from the ground and slits the Mayor's throat, finishing the job. I stand, leaning against a nearby tree for support just before the light leaves the Devilin's eyes. She turns to face the rest of the Dreads, and takes a step toward them. Fear filling their eyes and they all run back into the deep forest. Nicki stands dumb founded at the sight of her fallen father. The Slayers chase them and Nicki run with her hosts, glancing back one last glare at Anika, revenge deep in her eyes, then she glances at me.

This isn't over. It's just the beginning. Her voice is a harsh whisper, but it leaves with her. Anika puts her hand on her stab wound, her face twists with pain; she slowly, yet gracefully, sinks to the ground. I hurry toward her dizzily and take her in my arms.

"You saved me," I say moving her hair out of her face. She opens her eyes, which to my relief are emerald green and not silver, and chuckles, followed by coughing.

"Well I had to return the favor. You've saved me more times than I can count." She says softly, smiling weakly. I smile back at her.

"What else is a guy to do if he doesn't have a beautiful young woman to save?" I reply chuckling and to my surprise her response is a kiss on the cheek. We both blush in shades of red so dark we look like we have bad sunburns. We are joined by her father after that, who looks at us both suspiciously at our blushes. He just shakes his head and kneels by his daughter.

"What happened Father? Why did I turn into," Anika doesn't finish her thought. Her father looks at her apologetically.

"I'm sorry Anika; I should have told you long ago that this would happen. I will explain everything later. Here, crush the plant and put it on your wound until we can go home and cure it properly." He instructs, placing a strange looking dark purple flower in Anika's hands.

"But, it's Aconitum. Doesn't it kill wolves?"

"Normally yes, but with Slayers it doesn't. Instead it sucks out the poison in silver. But it smells bad to Slayers because of its potency." Her father replies turning to go find Jackson. She does as her father instructed, clenching her jaw in pain once it touches the wound. She growls, her eyes flashing silver and she snaps at me. To my surprise, I jump out of range from her teeth and she falls to the ground, knocking her back to her senses.

"Oh my gosh! I'm so sorry! I don't know what happened!" She says cowering on the ground; I approach her cautiously until I see her eyes are green again. I slowly help her to her feet.

"It's okay; I understand you didn't do it on purpose. I do have the combined blood of your natural enemy. I'd be surprised if you didn't attack me." I say lightly. That's when Jackson comes sprinting from the forest looking panicked, his eyes are silver.

"Anika, hurry. They have your father! They're pointing a gun at him. You need to run; they're coming for you too." He says before he transforms and runs the opposite direction from where he came. She starts to walk where we saw her father go; I grab her arm to stop her. She turns to face me, fear in her eyes.

"We have to help him."

Chapter 19: Alpha

-Anika

I half limp half run to my father, somehow can sense exactly where he is. Xander stays by my side, helping me if I stumble. I look toward the sky as the sun light starts growing telling us that morning has arrived. When we reach him we find him tied with rope entwined with threads of silver. He's surrounded by wounded town's men. One in the middle that seems to be the group's leader holds a gun pointed at my father's heart.

The leader speaks sternly in a low, serious voice. "You don't know how long I've been waiting for you. Now you practically served yourself up on a silver platter to me." My father growls at him, and I begin to recognize the figure. He was tall, muscular, and blonde with gray hair speckled through it. Coach Dastin stands with a silver gun, his face blank but his brown eyes filled with determination. I'm in shock. "The town of Wolfsbane is done with this strange monster stuff. They have started training monster hunters on their own, just like you were teaching Anika. Oh yes, we know all about that. And we are going to put a stop to both the Dreads, and the Slayers. No more scary monsters threatening our town anymore."

He slowly pulls the trigger. "I'm sorry, Deputy Conall- but it must be done." He says I hear a bang; everything goes dull in my eardrums. I don't hear myself scream, but I feel Xander grab me around my waist as I try launching myself at Coach Dastin. He turns, surprised at my scream but his face remains expressionless. My father sinks to his knees, and then falls limp against the tree. Dastin shoots him again, in the head. I look at the football coach with hatred.

"You monster! What have you done! He protected you! Helped the town! Why would you do this?" I cry, suddenly feeling weak.

"Sure he helped us, but he is a monster, like the Dreaded. He'd turn on us eventually, for power, or food. You remember what happened to your ancestors. The Slayer went in the forest and then they were never seen again. They're killers

Anika. We must destroy them, or by destroyed by them." He lifts his gun at me, Xander stiffens.

"If you shoot that gun, you will go down within seconds." Xander challenges. Coach Dastin's brown eyes are cold. He nods at Marcus, one of his men who points one of my father's guns that shoots Copper bullets at Xander, Marcus smiles at the shift in power he has against Xander.

"Since you helped us, I will give you a head start of five seconds to run then come after you until you are dead. Pity that two of most promising, talented young women in this town turn out to be monsters," His followers cut the rope that holds my father to the tree and he flops lifelessly to the ground. "One, two," Dastin begins counting, I feel numb inside, Xander grabs my hand and pulls me into the forest in full sprint. I follow feeling more dead than alive. "Three, four," his voice echoes hauntingly through the trees. We sprint faster, dodging trees, logs, and lifeless Dreads. "FIVE!" He shouts. They come after us, shooting when they catch a glimpse of us, but missing every time. Soon Xander becomes more alert.

"Get ready to jump! Now!" He commands, but I don't realize it in time. I jump too late with little force. Xander lands gracefully on the other side of a large cliff, but I am free falling into a steep, rocky ravine. My stomach is in my throat and sudden panic rises within me. I hit the edge hard and Xander grabs me and pulls me up and into his arms and hides behind a nearby tree. He gives me the 'be quiet, don't move' signal by placing his finger on his lips and we listen for the mob. It sounds like one of Dastin's companions almost falls off the edge when we can finally hear them, but he's caught.

"Don't be an idiot Marcus; watch where you're going or you'll get yourself killed." Dastin's harsh voice said. "Looks like they either crossed or turned and ran the other way, let's head back, we can't cross the ravine without being killed anyway." I hear footsteps until all is quiet. My nerves can't take the shock anymore. I start crying silently, which slowly turns to bawling as the shock and adrenaline wear off. *My father is dead, I don't know where my mother is, I can't go home or back to town without getting shot at, I'm part monster, and I'm stuck in the woods with no food or water and no where to go. I'm lost, scared and don't know what to do.* My thoughts over whelm me and Xander just holds me, not saying anything, stroking my hair.

We stand like that for a long time until I'm quiet. Then he speaks, "Are you alright?" I shake my head, but say nothing. "How's your wound?" I totally forgot about it, but it feels fine. I still say nothing; he tilts my chin so I'm looking into his eyes. "Anika, I know you're upset. But please, talk to me. I'll go crazy if you don't." his golden eyes plead to mine.

"I'll be fine. We need to get moving." I say quietly, looking deep into his eyes.

"Oh thank goodness! You can speak! I was afraid you had gone mute or something!" He chuckles softly; I can't help but give a weak small smile that quickly slipped away. He frowns, trying to figure out a way to make me happy. "I'm just glad that you're alive. When they took you, I didn't know what to do. I felt so helpless." he shakes his head.

"Why did you care so much?" I ask quietly.

"You're my best friend Anika, you mean more to me than you realize." He sighs, "I have such strong feelings for you." I raise an eyebrow.

"What do you mean?"

"Stop playing oblivious with me Anika, It's extremely obvious." He looks away from me shyly but his arms tighten around me bringing me closer to him. I get a strange nervous, tingly feeling inside me- a glimmer of hope amidst all of the pain.

"Xander, I…" I don't know how to respond, my head spun and I am bleeding so my thoughts aren't clear. I'm not sure how I feel.

"I understand- it isn't the right time. You've been through a lot. We should get moving." He says starting to walk when he pauses. "Where are we going? We've been basically exiled from Wolfsbane on pain of death. We have no food, survival kit. What do we do?"

"We must find shelter, I have a feeling we should travel north. We must stay away from the West, that's where Wolfsbane is. The East is nothing but forest. And the South is where the Dreads ran to. It's also where their hide out is." Xander nods at this as if he remembered something.

"I remember Nicki say something about not crossing a river into Slayer territory. She said if I did they'd kill me. Basically, where ever I go, they will kill me."

"They will have to go through me if they want to kill you." I assure him walking north, he follows.

"The river that divides the territories is this way." He tells me, walking ahead. That's when I hear leaves shuffling; I look around us, scanning the trees. I can see muscular figures surround us that are hiding, I stiffen. Xander notices them too, and stops moving. "We need to get out of here. It's an ambush."

"They're not her to fight, they're hungry. They want to kill us because their animal instincts tell them too. Nicki isn't here to control them or they'd be stealthier, just run." I instruct. He takes off, and I do the same right on his heels.

I can hear the snow crunch under my feet as I run, I run as fast as I can. I try to leave my past behind me, but it seems to follow me. I can never escape it. Now my father is dead, my mother disappeared and now only my best friend, Xander and I are running in the forest together trying to escape the horrible things that follow us. I'm terrified, something stirs within me, the animal inside me is clawing its way to the surface. I force it back into its cage before it takes control. *We were betrayed and exiled into the one place we won't live for long. There is no one to save us, I'm not sure we can even save ourselves.*

I duck under a branch, it scratches my face and I bleed a little, making the creatures chasing us more wild and hungry. Adrenaline is the only thing keeping me going now. My breathing is hurried and I pick up speed. The beating of my heart is the only noise I hear other than the growls of the monsters behind us. Memories flash in my mind, a copper knife pressed against Xander's throat, and one of my teachers with a gun pointed at my father. I shake my head to rid the memory from my mind.

    The growls of the monsters are becoming louder and more persistent. I know that there are more of them than I originally thought. I don't know how much longer I can keep running, my legs are going numb. I look at Xander, who is in the lead. He jumps over a log but I don't see it. My shin hits the frozen log and I fall on my face. I'm cold, tired, starving, and now I'm angry. Xander slides to a stop and runs over to me, but it's too late. The creatures surround us but this time I'm not worried. I let the beast out of the cage. I look up at Xander; he takes a step back from me feeling uneasy. I swallow my own fear and let it take over. They deserve this; they will regret everything they've done.

    I tackle one, snarling, using my claws to cut at its throat, it falls limp instantly. They keep coming, there are about thirty of them. I feel weak;

my wound feels like it's on fire. There are too many for me to take down at once.

"Anika, cross the river, they can't touch us if we cross it, they wouldn't dare." I hear Xander shout behind me. I take his word for it, we walk through the river, I'm still in this monster form. The Dreads back away, and we watch them cower and run off, disappearing into their side of the forest, one stops and hisses at us before following the others. "That was close." Xander sighs. I turn to see that we aren't why the Dreads have run off.

Behind us was a huge Pack of Slayers. Xander stiffens the white Slayer steps forward. "Artemis," he woofs in wolf speak. My ears perk up. No one has called me by my first name in years since I was a child. Not even my parents called me by it.

"How do you know me?" I growls back in wolf language.

"It's me, Asher. Asher Ulric. We used to be friends before the Alpha took you to Wolfsbane." He explains, and then he looks at Xander and growls menacingly, as do the rest of the Slayers, I move in front of Xander, standing protectively between him and the Pack.

"I remember you, vaguely. Don't hurt the human. He's traveling with me."

"That thing is not human."

"He's a hybrid, but he is on our side, and he's my best friend. No one will harm him. If you do, I will unleash the same thing you did to him to you ten fold. Do we have an understanding?"

"Indeed we do. Where is the Alpha, is he with you?"

"Alpha? Who is the Alpha?"

"You're father Artemis, where is he?"

"He's… dead, killed by the town's people's Hunters. They tried to get us to but we escaped." Asher ponders this for a moment before turning away.

"Follow us; we will take you to the Caves. We have a lot to discuss." Asher says, but before he continues, he howls a loud, long, sad howl. The rest of the pack does the same, and then they slowly walk North, following Asher with their heads down and tails between their legs. I turn human and grab Xander's hand.

"They won't hurt you. They're taking us to shelter, just follow them okay?" He nods and we follow them quietly through the forest. It seems to take forever until we come out of the trees to see a huge lake and beyond it, mountains, and huge mountains. The people in Wolfsbane called them Thunder Ridge because of all of the lightning that strikes here and the booming thunder that echoes off the mountain side.

The pack of Slayers turn into humans dressed in jeans and black t-shirts, walking toward hand made canoes on the edge of the lake. Asher: the tall, handsome, dirty blonde boy with gray eyes on the bridge of his nose from my dream strolls next to us. "Luna Lake." He says as we near the wooden canoes. "Just beyond it are the Caves, or what we call Home."

We get into a canoe and row across the lake in silence. The sun has risen in the sky suggesting that it's about nine in the morning now. I feel drowsy and rest my head on a bench while Xander and Asher row and fall asleep. I can hear everything that is going on even though I am asleep.

"Her wound looks bad; we need to get her to Bones- he'll know what to do. What kind of knife was it?"

"Silver"

"Then we must hurry." Xander wakes me when we get to the other end of the Lake, by then all energy has failed me. He carries me into the caves and follows Asher. I am too exhausted to open my eyes, so I don't see where they take me. "Set her down here, I'll go get Bones. Cole, Twigs- you stay here and guard them until I get back."

I hear Asher leave but Xander never leaves my side, he holds me in his arms and won't let go. I don't mind, it's the most comforting thing about the whole situation especially since he is the only one I trust currently. His fingers trace my face; I don't stir but feel a warm tingly feeling that his fingers leave behind on my skin. I hear nothing but silence until two pairs of footsteps echo around me, Xander's grip tightens slightly around me protectively.

"Is this really her?" an unfamiliar tenor voice asks,

"Yes, this is the Alpha's daughter."

"Stabbed by Silver you say?"

"Yes, in her left side."

"She has to drink this elixir to rid the poison. It will take time to heal."

"Thank you Bones, you are always a lifesaver." Asher says graciously. I feel my head tilt up and hear Xander's sweet voice whisper, "This will make you better. You have to drink it. But I warn you that it smells awful." He opens my mouth and pours the sludge in. It tastes of dirt and smells of dead plants. I swallow, coughing until the bitter taste numbs my mouth. Soon my senses dull until I hear and see nothing.

Epilogue
-Anika

Everything is fuzzy, distant. I hear someone call my name, but it seems far away. My side throbs, I groan. My eyes burst open, the darkness that surrounds me is so thick I feel like I'm being suffocated. Flashes of light appear in front of my vision, like a vivid memory. I see my father slump against the tree he's tied to, his eyes lifeless and cold. I scream, but I can't hear anything, I feel as if I'm in water and things sound distant and muffled and I can't seem to move very fast. "Monster," *Dastin spits at my father lowering the gun he holds in his hands. Then he turns to me, and I realize it isn't Coach Dastin. It's Mayor Rune.* "You're the monster." *I feel a growl rise in my throat, the Mayor cocks the gun at me but it's too late. I lunge at him allowing the monster to take over I jump on him, knocking the gun from his hands. But instead of the Mayor, it's now Xander.* "Anika, please. I'm not you're enemy. I'm you're friend! Please remember! Anika come back! Come back!" *I lean down to his neck not even bothering to think of anything else but biting the life out of my enemy, the Dreaded. "Anika, come back to me!"*

Xander's voice echoes in my head and I wake up screaming. I'm in a cold sweat, my side aches and my head and heart are pounding. My breathing is ragged and I feel exposed, exhausted, and alone. I cough, a fowl taste envelopes my mouth. I feel like I might puke. It was all just a bad dream. My fears placed out I front of me, my mind processing what just happened. I'm crying now, from the shock or the fear I'm not sure. I'm shaking, I need to calm down. Obviously I'm scarred by my father's cold blooded murder and the fact that I am a monster inside that's a sworn enemy to my best friend. I don't want to hurt him; he's the only one I have now. I sit up slowly and allow my mind to try and calm down by processing what was going on.

I'm all alone in the darkness. The hole inside me has grown with the loss of my family and all I want is for Xander to come and hold me, as pathetic as that sounds, it's the truth. I claw at the dirt on the ground, feeling confused and anxious to disappear or have the ground swallow me whole and numb the pain. I growl, a fowl taste and residue was still in my mouth from the strange tonic they'd given me earlier- the stench is very strong. I gag and roll on my side and spit it out, trying to rid the taste from my mouth. I was hungry, alone, and miserable. Why would Xander leave me like this? Eventually I know I need to move, hunger claws at my stomach angrily. I sit up slowly; a deep dull pain resonates where I had been stabbed. I suck in a large breath and whimper as I put my hand on the wound, putting pressure on it that seems to lessen the pain. Movement in the corner of the room causes me to look in its direction. It was too dark to see anything, I heard two stones scrape together and sparks flew catching on to something and burst into a large flame that lit the room. I am blinded by the sudden burst of light and shield my eyes, allowing them to adjust.

"Finally, Sleeping Beauty is awake! Gave us quiet a scare you did." A girl's voice says, I watch her with uncertainty with distrust. "I'm Amber; it's nice to finally meet you Artemis. I've heard so much about you." She says standing up and walking to my side. As my eyes adjust I realize she is the long, curly haired, red head girl from the dream I had a while ago.

"Who told you about me?" I ask stiffly, removing my hand from my eyes.

"Asher did, and the Moon told him about you, the Moon tells him lots of things, especially bits of the future that matter. But he isn't the true Alpha, the Alpha is dead. You told us and Asher says that the Moon confirms it."

"The moon?"

"Hasn't the Alpha told you about that, about any of this?"

"No, he never said anything."

"So, he hasn't told you that the Moon picked you as his replacement?" I stiffen, my face fills with shock.

"What?" I squeak in response.

"I guess not… I probably shouldn't have said anything. I'm so sorry! I'll take you to Asher so he can explain everything. Come, this way."

Made in the USA
San Bernardino, CA
03 May 2014